# UNFINISHED SEDUCTIONS

RALEIGH DAVIS

# CHAPTER 1

My roses are pissing me off.

The petals are too uniform, the centers too vague, and the leaves aren't curling right. But it isn't the roses' fault they're imperfect—as the artist, all the blame lies with me.

The roses growing outside my tiny painting shed are the kind of art that only life itself can do. I rented this house specifically for the garden, with its ancient plants growing high and wild, stone paths cutting through it like fairy trails, and the greenhouse converted into an artist's studio. I thought I could finally *create* here, like I haven't in years.

But the roses in my watercolors aren't even close. Some days I can get this aspect or the other of them captured on my canvas, and I keep trying to grab all of them, but this painting...

It sucks.

I set the watercolor pad aside, cover my paints, and leave my brushes to soak. The roses don't have to be painted. I can simply let them be. I didn't come to this place to get frustrated all over again with my life. I came here to hide and to do what I couldn't back in the Valley, caught there in a world and a marriage I didn't understand.

I didn't do watercolors back then. No, the titans of the tech world only want simple, bright, bold for their logos and from their graphic designers, which is what I'd once been.

No, I still am. I shake my head. I might be Logan Martell's wife, but I was something before that too. That didn't go away.

A graphic designer wouldn't paint in watercolors. She'd have a graphics tablet in her hand, creating with pixels and programs. If she did pick actual pens or brushes to put to actual paper, it'd be ink or acrylics. Bold, masculine tools to create designs with.

Watercolors are girly. Which is why I've been doing nothing but them since I left Logan. I needed art that was as far away from him and his world as possible.

I tug my sweater over my hands and push my shoulders up by my ears, trying to capture some warmth. The garden is picturesque but also freezing in the mornings.

Enough painting for today. I don't need to open the french doors into my little cottage because I've already left them open. It's cool here, way up in Platina, Northern California, and always damp, but I leave the windows open as much as I can. I want to let the real world into my life even if it's uncomfortable. Being uncomfortable is a novel luxury after my marriage.

The cottage is a tiny house built before they became all the rage. It's one room basically, with a bathroom and closet in their own nooks and a bed in a loft above. I feel cozy here because it *is* so small. There's no empty space for me to rattle around in.

Meowthra uncurls on his window perch and yawns as I come in.

The owner explained that the cat came with the house. "He comes, he goes, he does as he pleases," he said. "That cat doesn't really belong to anyone."

That's fine by me since I can understand that attitude. Meowthra is more of a roommate than a pet, keeping to his own schedule and disappearing for hours at a time to do his own thing. I leave some food and water for him and give him pets when he allows it. He never asks for them though, which is something I can respect. If I hadn't begged for love myself, I wouldn't be in this mess.

I plug in the electric kettle and pull out everything I need for a sandwich. After failing to capture the roses all morning, I'm starving. And I think—I can't quite remember—I skipped breakfast.

When I pull out the tuna, Meowthra deigns to wrap himself around my ankles, begging for some. In the battle between dignity and tuna, tuna would always win for him.

I bend down to give him a spoonful—he wouldn't eat it out of his bowl—and as I do, the knock comes at the front door, the one door in the house that's shut.

I jump up so suddenly Meowthra yowls like I stepped on him and streaks out the back door, which is open.

"Jeez." I grab the countertop to steady myself. I occasionally get visitors—after being here a few months, I've made some friends in town, and some people from my old life, like Julian, make the trek to see me—so I shouldn't jump like I touched a hot stove.

"What the hell?"

When I hear that voice come through the door, I immediately understand why I reacted the way I did. Somehow my subconscious recognized that knock. It knew who was on the other side of that door.

He knocks again. "Callie?"

I hold my breath, pretending to be dead or gone or just plain nonexistent. If I don't move, he won't hear me. And I won't have to talk to him, won't have to confront my failures with him.

The doorknob rattles.

He's not fooled. But then, Logan's always been the smartest person I know.

"Callie?" It's a question but also a demand to be let in. "What did I hear? Are you okay?"

The concern in his voice hits me right in the knees. And the gut. When he was focused on me, there was no one who'd ever loved me better, not even my mother.

And when his focus left me, alone and cold…

"I'm fine," I say as I push off from the countertop. My knees wobble, but they hold. My stomach wobbles even harder, but I don't have to worry about it holding me up. "I'm coming."

I've managed to hide from him for almost four months now, a remarkable achievement considering his wealth and power. I had help, of course, but I'm still amazed I made it this long.

I knew from the moment I ran that he'd catch up with me one day. Not because he believes I'm his possession or to drag me back like a caveman—no, I didn't leave Logan because he'd been abusive or even mean or because I'd stopped loving him. I left because I loved him too much.

And I know he's been looking for me. My mother and Julian know where I am, but they swore to never tell him, not that it would stop Logan. The fact that a PI hasn't appeared on my doorstep already is shocking.

Maybe Logan knew all along where I was and he's only now decided to meet me face-to-face. Julian keeps telling me that Logan's asked about me, that I need to contact a lawyer and start the divorce. I never did, although I can't explain why.

Maybe Logan's here to talk about the divorce. My stomach cramps so hard I can't breathe for a moment.

I'm going to have to face him. Confront the ruins of our marriage.

The door opens too fast, revealing him like a slap. He's...

I bite my lip, my breath coming hard and rapid. He's always been handsome, beautiful, gorgeous, all the words you could ever put on male beauty. It's not just his sharp cheekbones, thick black hair, or pouting mouth—it's his intensity. When a will that powerful looks out through navy-blue eyes in a face like his, you're powerless.

At least I *was*. I won't be anymore though.

"Callie." He sets a forearm against the doorjamb, as if he's exhausted. He does look wrecked, his skin too sallow and his forehead too tight, but it's a beautiful wreckage. Trust Logan to look heart-wrenchingly sad instead of awfully sad.

"Are you okay? What was that?"

"The cat." My hand trembles on the door. Maybe I can slam it, hide away again, never have to face the wreckage...

I swallow hard. I never used to be a shrinking violet. I used to be, if not exactly bold, at least unafraid. If I'm going to survive without him—like really without him instead of simply running away from him—I've got to be brave enough to talk to him. Brave enough to end things and break my own heart.

I open the door wider. He's come a long way, and I can't slam the door on him. Seeing him after so long... I'm addicted all over again. "You should come in."

I don't want to talk, but I know we have to. I ran so I wouldn't have to face him, but he's found me, so I owe him at least that.

He hesitates on the porch, his gaze running over me. It's like having the sun look at me—bright, hot, and too much.

"If you're sure." His voice is as gorgeous as the rest of him, deep but smooth as silk. Dark chocolate without the bitterness. I want to lick up every drop, even now.

I step back and let him in. I don't know what he'll make of my cottage, so different from the house we shared in San Francisco. That place was practically an estate high on Twin Peaks, overlooking the entire city. It even had *grounds*, with a lawn and a garden and a gazebo. Places in the City, even the most expensive ones, don't usually have that much space. But Logan did. He can command things other people can only dream of.

Logan walks in after me but says nothing. His gaze stays on me, which means he isn't even seeing the cottage.

That's the thing about his focus. It's so intense it's flattering—and almost *flatten*ing—but it's also singular. If you're in its path, it's great. But if you're outside, it's like you don't even exist to him.

When we first married, I was right there in the center. Then slowly, slowly I was pushed out of his orbit. Until I was invisible and freezing in my own marriage.

I wait for him to speak first, mostly because I can't think of where to start. I didn't fantasize about this meeting because I didn't want to face it even in my imagination. I never knew I was so good at hiding, even from myself.

Maybe that's why I never contacted a lawyer or initiated divorce proceedings. I didn't want to imagine seeing him again and facing the end of my marriage. And if I didn't imagine it, it couldn't happen.

I didn't want to go on as we were, but I also didn't want my marriage to end.

He lifts his palms, his mouth twisting. But nothing comes out.

I wrap my arms around myself. Suddenly I wish I'd closed the windows and all the doors, pulled all the curtains closed, and sealed myself in the cottage.

"Why are you here?" I ask. Might as well get the hard

conversation over with. Even so, I brace myself to hear the *D* word.

He looks like he can't believe what I just asked. "You're my *wife*." He makes it sound like I've stolen something from him. But I belong to myself—I can't steal myself.

"Am I?" I ask softly. The question is meant for me more than him.

"I'm here because..." He swallows hard, choking something down. His voice is as rigid as his stance. Like he's trying to hold back a volcano of emotion. "Did you think I wouldn't look for you? That I wouldn't come for you when I found you?"

He makes it sound like he's come to save me. Even if I don't want to be saved.

"I wasn't kidnapped," I say. "I chose to leave. And not to contact you."

Logan lifts his hands again, the gesture helpless. "Why?" he finally asks. "Just... why?"

I shake my head. "I... I can't explain it."

His expression hardens. "Was it Julian?"

Of course it can't be Logan's fault. It has to be some outside force, which is why I can't explain *why* to him. It'd be like explaining the color blue to someone who has never seen it before.

And it *was* Julian, but not how he thinks. Julian is my friend, has been for a long time, and nothing more. He's a venture capitalist like Logan, and when I realized I needed to leave, I knew I'd need help. After being dependent on Logan for so long, there were so many things to prepare for— money, a house, utilities—everything that Logan had used to take care of for me.

"Julian is my friend," I say. "I've told you that before. Many times."

His expression never changes. "You left with him. You

said to contact you through him. You never said anything to me, and he…" His eyes darken with rage. "He fucking flaunts it."

That sounds like Julian. He's never warmed to Logan, and since they're competitors, he'd want to get some digs in.

"I didn't leave *with* him." I'm getting angry too, the hot pulse of it loosening my arms, pursing my lips. "He helped me find a place to stay—and he wasn't staying with me."

"Fine." I can tell he doesn't believe me though. Logan is as intense in his jealousy as he is in everything else. "But again: Why? I gave you everything—"

I cut him off right there. "How long did it take for you to notice I was gone?"

His shoulders sag, and he runs a hand over his face. He's wearing a heavy coat, and it's scattered with mist, twinkling in the light from the windows. "I was frantic when I realized."

Which isn't an answer at all. "My mother knew where I was. Julian knew where I was. So did all my friends."

He slices me a look. "And you told them not to tell me. They said I wasn't to contact you."

I can only guess how intimidating he must have been, demanding answers from them. They'd held strong anyway.

"Then how did you find me? A PI?"

His lip curls. "You said you wanted me to stay away, so I stayed away, like a perfect *gentleman*. Finally your mother said something."

"My mother told you?" Mom is an old-school feminist who tried to raise me in her radical, bra-burning image. I went in this marriage so full of hopes, ready to prove her wrong: *Look, a marriage can last. Two people can be equals. Logan and I will be equals.*

I'd loved Logan desperately, and I thought love would be enough. That we'd forge this perfect, transcendent marriage, free of our parents' baggage, because our love was just that strong.

But it wasn't, and my mom hated Logan in the end for hurting me. Not all her lessons took, but she's the last person I expected to take Logan's side.

"Why would she tell you?" After holding out for so long, it didn't make sense.

His smile is so bitter my mouth aches. "Because I told her the magic word."

Everything slows and the seconds stutter as they tick by. Because I know exactly what word he's referring to.

So this is it. This is the end.

We met when Bastard Capital, the venture capital firm he runs with five of his closest friends, wanted to rebrand and update their logo from the do-it-yourself one they'd put together back when they were all working in a garage. They were just out of college then, having hit it rich with a stock-price prediction program.

By the time I met them, they were major movers and shakers in the tech world and wanted their brand imagery to reflect that. So they hired the design firm I worked for, and I was the lucky designer they'd been assigned.

The Bastards are all attractive and all very rich, but I wasn't moved by that. My firm wasn't cheap, and I was used to meeting the demands of young billionaires.

But Logan... Logan was like no other man I'd ever encountered.

When his eyes first met mine, I felt like I couldn't fill my lungs. Like if I didn't kiss him, I was never going to breathe again. Which is over the top, yes, but so is love. And that's how we fell for each other—intense and fast and gasping for breath.

Once we were married, when I knew he loved me, I felt

like I could inhale again. Like my every breath was full and pure.

But that's the problem with loving someone so much you need them to breathe: when they leave the marriage behind, you suffocate. And that's exactly what I did for the last year of our marriage.

These past few months without him, I relearned how to breathe on my own. It wasn't fun—it was downright painful—and while I'm not exactly happy, I'm no longer miserable. I've found equilibrium, shaky as it is.

Or at least I thought I had. "You mean…"

His smile grows too bitter for him to hold it. "That's right. Divorce."

## CHAPTER 2

I've spent the past few months not understanding.

Not understanding why Callie would leave, why she'd flee like that, why only Julian could speak to her and I couldn't...

Now that I've found her, I still don't understand. I love her, so badly it's killing me, and she looks like she wishes she'd never seen me. Never married me.

I've always found it difficult to look away from her, from the first moment I saw her. Not only because she's beautiful but because I *recognized* something in her. Call it déjà vu, kindred spirits, soul mates, but it was real.

I don't recognize her now. Her features are all the same— hazel eyes that refuse to be any one color; soft, wide mouth that always gives away her inner state; and high cheekbones that make her look more somber than she actually is. But her features are arranged in an expression so distant I wonder if we're even in the same room here.

The bomb I've just thrown between us has blasted us even further apart.

"Oh." Callie sinks down onto the sofa built into the wall, only big enough for two. This place she's holed up in is tiny, too small for more than one person. But maybe that was the point.

"Isn't that what you wanted? That's what you told Julian." His name can't come out of my mouth as anything but a snarl. "Can you at least tell me why you left? I'm at least owed that much."

"Did you ever think that going on as we had been was making me miserable?" She tucks her hands deeper into her sweater as if she wants to disappear into it. The sweater is oversized, the yarn thick and lumpy. It falls past her hips, the sleeves cover her hands, and the cowl goes up to her chin. It's more like armor than anything cozy.

"Miserable?" I can't even understand the word coming from her. She never wanted for anything. The house, her car, her clothes—she didn't even have to work anymore. The entire world was at her fingertips, thanks to my wealth. "You could have done anything you wanted. You still can. If you want to work instead of the charity stuff—"

Her hands curl into fists. I can see the lumps of them in her sleeves. "No, that's... My mother warned me what would happen, and she was right. I just... I don't belong in that world. Your world."

Her hair, a curtain of shimmering golds and browns, swings forward to hide her face. She's let it grow long, past her shoulder blades. Her hand, bare of the rings and the watch I gave her, reaches up to tuck it back.

I can reach out and brush her cheek, take her hand. This house is so small there's nowhere for her to go where she isn't within arm's reach of me. The air between us is buzzing, snapping, coming alive with the awareness that only we share. If I could just touch her, like I'm aching to—

My gaze cuts away. "Of course you belong. I built that world for you." Does she think I work like a demon only for myself? I do it for her so that she'll never have to worry again, not like my mother did.

I also did it because Callie is the very first woman I've ever looked at and thought *home.* A sensation so bright and pure I would have destroyed anything that threatened her or it. The more money I made, the safer she was.

Her shoulders slump. "Can you remember the last time we spent time together? *Real* time together, not just passing each other in the hall?"

I pull up my memories of the past few months, ready to contradict her... but I can't. Work has been intense, requiring all my attention.

Her smile when I don't answer is sad, which makes me feel stupid and angry all over again.

"Logan..." She lifts her palms, exhales. "You're the most focused person I know. And all your focus is for your work."

That focus is what makes me an asset to the Bastards—I can buckle down and train a laser eye on a project. For hours. Days. Weeks. When you're dealing with computer code or multimillion-dollar deals in a lightning-fast industry, that's a huge plus.

"You're focused too," I say. It's what attracted me to her—that intensity in her that I recognized in myself. With me, my focus becomes an obsession, but Callie transforms her focus into passion.

"Not like you. With you, it's a sickness."

Chills run down my back like I'm catching a fever. She always could read me too well. "It's not. Being distracted, inattentive, unable to do a job—that's a sickness. A weakness."

"Logan, I know how you feel about your dad."

Obviously not, or she wouldn't have said what she did. My jaw clenches back angry words.

My father died a failure. Never able to hold down a job,

always jumping from one get-rich-quick scheme to another, throwing his entire self into one failure after another. He didn't leave anything behind for my mother except never-ending stress and struggle.

I'm not going to end up like him. And if anything happens to me, I'm going to make damn sure Callie doesn't end up like my mom.

But that isn't what Callie wants to hear. I know how this script should go: I say, "You're right. I'm working too much. Let's take a vacation, take time together. And I promise I'll cut back on my hours when we get back."

And in that script, she believes me, wraps me up in one of her hugs, and I take her back where she belongs.

Except that role was written for someone else. Not me.

Just the thought of saying that makes sweat gather under my shirt, cold from the damp air coming in through the windows. Why the hell is she leaving the windows open?

"Callie. You—" I stop, make my voice obey me. "You know I work hard to provide for you. I don't do it because I don't want to be with you. I do it because I want you to have everything."

She wets her lower lip. "I don't want you to change. I know you can't, and I know why. But I realized I can't be the kind of wife you need."

My scalp tingles when she says *wife*. There's something off there, but I can't understand what.

"Can you give me a real answer?" I say. "And not any more bullshit."

She's exactly the kind of wife I need, or at least the Callie she'd been before had been. But this stranger isn't the Callie I fell in love with.

Her hands are gripping each other tightly. Her hair falls forward again, and this time she doesn't push it back. "I should have said something." She shakes her head. "Not that it would have helped. You have trouble admitting you're wrong."

I can definitely admit I'm wrong. It just happens so rarely though. And I wasn't wrong about us. At least not about how we were in the beginning.

She doesn't seem to want an apology or promises of change or anything from me. She seems to only want me to go.

Anger surges in me, at myself for not being able to stick to the script she wants about working less and changing more and at her for becoming this woman I don't recognize. Anger that she simply left rather than telling me anything. How could she give up on me? On us?

Even now, the pull between us is potent, although it's dark and twisted like it never was.

"You want me to admit I'm wrong?" I reach into my jacket pocket and pull out the thick envelope. I toss it to the table before her. "Here. I was wrong. About you, me, our marriage... Here's your chance to erase it all."

"Did Elliot draw those up?" She's staring at the envelope as if it's a scorpion, her knees pulling up toward her belly.

Elliot is our lawyer, a partner in Bastard Capital, and my brother. I know what she's thinking—Elliot's screwed her over here. For some reason she and Elliot never got along.

Maybe I would have taken that as a warning sign if I hadn't been so love drunk.

"He did."

"Elliot always hated me." She barely moves her lips to get that out.

I shake my head. "Elliot insisted I give you half. I didn't even have to bring it up." I look out the window, at the low clouds blotting out the sun. "Which includes half my shares in Bastard Capital."

There was a massive brawl about that, with Mark

insisting that legally there had to be a way out, Elliot muttering about the prenup I refused to let him draw up, and Paul telling me all the stories of the gold diggers who married into his family.

Finn just looked sick to his stomach, and Dev... Dev was Dev. Quiet and controlled as ever.

But I can't leave Callie with less than half. The thought of her struggling through the world, working at some shit job she hated, when I could give her enough to never worry again...

The shares of Bastard Capital will only increase in value. They'll be her insurance against the world, better than cash.

"And if she sells them?" Mark demanded. "Then we have some asshole from outside in our fucking business."

"She won't," I said. "Not unless she's desperate."

Mark knew then there was no more point arguing with me. They all did.

I got Elliot to write everything up, then came here, feeling like I was carrying a grenade with the pin pulled.

"I can't take those shares," she says. Then she catches herself, putting her fingers over her lips.

"We're not arguing about this." I shove my hands in my pockets to give myself something to do other than reaching for her. "It's all yours."

She looks like I've yelled at her rather than handing her a several-billion-dollar fortune. "Oh, Logan." The disappointment there confuses me all over again.

I can't do this any longer, or otherwise I'll grab those divorce papers and burn them. I have to get out of this too-small house, away from this woman who looks exactly like Callie but acts like a stranger. "I've gotta go. I'm staying at a place in town tonight if you need to reach me. In the morning I'm heading back to the City."

Her gaze flickers as she looks at me. "The Hideaway Inn? But it's so... poky."

I shrug. "I've stayed in worse places."

"Not lately."

She's right, but the sagging beds and stained walls at the Hideaway suit my mood. "There isn't much to choose from."

One motel, two restaurants, and no grocery store. Not even the tourists wander this far north.

She lifts a hand to indicate her sofa, then lets it drop.

I give her a wistful smile. No, my staying here won't work for a lot of reasons, but it's so like Callie to offer anyway. The old Callie, that is.

My chest constricts too tight to breathe for a moment.

I leave before the image of me and her tangled together in that loft bed embeds any deeper in my mind.

## CHAPTER 3

I stare at the envelope on the table as if it's a viper Logan's tossed at me.

When I shouted that stuff about getting a lawyer at Mark, I wasn't sure if I actually meant it. Julian was going on about how I needed to contact Logan, to start the legal proceedings, to move forward with my life, but I kept insisting I wasn't ready. I went into the City on that trip to get some stuff out of storage and deal with a few financial loose ends, not file for divorce.

And then Mark appeared and gotten in my face about Logan, and I said that to get him off my back. I never meant it, not really.

Elliot must have been gleeful while he drew up those papers. At least as gleeful as he gets, which was probably only a twitch of a smile. I don't think I've ever met two more different brothers. Elliot was just as intense as Logan, but he made it cold. Scary. You never got the feeling with Elliot you were the only person in the room—only that you were a severe annoyance.

If I touch those papers, all the Bastards' anger at me

would seep into my skin, make me sick. They never liked me before, but they must hate me now.

Shares in their precious VC firm. I can hardly believe they allowed Logan to offer those. Their bond goes tighter than brothers, and letting me have a piece of that bond when I divorce Logan is going to infuriate all of them.

I've seen how ruthless they are to their enemies. And I'll be one of those enemies if I take those shares.

I'm still staring at the envelope when Meowthra pokes his head back in, his expression accusing.

"Sorry. I didn't want him here either."

*Want.* It's the wrong word, because part of me did want him. Even now, my nerves are shimmering and popping, lit up because he was near. My body's been in hibernation since I left him, but right now it's very awake.

I needed that hibernation, the same way you need sleep to heal, but now that I'm awake… God, I hurt all over again.

Finally I snatch up the envelope. No better way to shut my body right back down than to look over some divorce papers.

I hold my breath as I leaf through all the legalese. It's not quite English, but I think I can translate well enough. Enough to see that Logan was telling the truth.

Half his every worldly good will be mine. Including his shares in Bastard Capital.

I try to envision myself walking into the Monday-morning partners' meeting, taking my place at the conference table. All of them would go nuclear, leaving a crater more radioactive than Fukushima.

Taking those shares… I force my lungs to empty. There's no way I can. I don't even want to take half his assets and the insane amount of alimony he's suggested. My mother would say take away from this marriage what I brought into it. Never be too dependent.

I used to tell her that emotional dependence was different, that it was *intimacy*, and that's what Logan and I had. That I could do the kinds of things all the other wives did but not lose myself in the role. Logan and I were better than that.

She was never dependent on anyone, not even my father. She'll say if she could do it twenty-some years ago, I can do it now.

But if I tell Logan no, that I don't want anything, he'll go ballistic. I know why, for the same reason why I know he won't change.

Logan's focused. Insanely so. And that focus includes his responsibilities, which includes me. If he thought I was struggling for money, working too hard and too long for too little, it would kill him.

His dad was the opposite of that, never focused enough to hold down a job, always wasting money they didn't have on his next big career move. His dad wasn't cruel or neglectful— just weak. But that weakness terrifies Logan. It's why he'll never slow down on work, not even for me.

It's probably why I ran from him. Because I was weak and I didn't want to see him pity me. Or worse, be repelled by me.

I carefully fold the divorce papers and put them back in the envelope, then put the envelope in a desk drawer. I don't even want to accidentally see them, not for a while. We've been apart for several months; I can wait to make a decision about a divorce.

Once that's done, I pull out my laptop.

When I was married to Logan, trying to fit in as the perfect Silicon Valley wife—not too well dressed, outdoorsy, very involved in her own personal charity foundation—I found myself slowly going mad. Those women were so smart, so accomplished in their own right... but they all fell into the exact same mold. It was like we were all getting fed into a machine stamping us out, obliterating our individuality. None of us, no matter how rich or determined, could escape it.

I thought I could try on the role for a while, see if it fit, then toss it aside if it didn't. But the more distant Logan became, the more I clung to that role, unable to let go.

My friends from before—arty, bohemian types—couldn't understand. I had money, which solved all problems, and wasn't I the one who'd chosen to marry the exact kind of man who was ruining *their* city? I never had to worry about rent hikes or eviction notices or hustling for freelance jobs until I collapsed with exhaustion. I might have sold out, but I also had it made.

They never said all those things straight out—they were still my friends—but they shot them in at an angle as I complained, blinking as they tried to understand where I was coming from now that I was so far above them economically.

Old friends, new friends, my husband—I had no one to talk to, *really* talk to.

So I started a blog. An anonymous one, somewhere to put down my observations and vent my feelings, safely concealed by the internet. I called it *The Silicon Wife*, which I thought was cute. No one read it.

Until one day someone did. And then another someone, and another. People that I knew. When the first of my acquaintances mentioned the blog, asking who might be behind it, I froze.

No one was ever supposed to read the thing. It was only for me.

When the next person brought it up, I was ready with a blank expression and questions of my own. *Who could be writing such a thing? How did she know all those inside details?*

She knew because *she* was me. Suddenly I was writing

one of the most popular gossip blogs in the Valley with everyone wondering who the hell I was.

I never told Logan. At that point he was at work more often than not. And by the time the blog got big, I hardly ever saw him. Besides, I wanted to keep my secret, to have my own tiny space within the marriage I was fighting so hard to fit into. I could be myself in my blog, without anyone watching. Or at least I could pretend no one was watching.

I've kept up with it while I was gone, although I never said that I ran away from Logan or even that I left him. That would have been a dead giveaway. Instead, I wrote vaguely about finding myself again, struggling with being lonely in my marriage, and who I really was. Mostly what I wrote about before, only sharper now that I was away from that world and could think about it without it looming over me.

Divorce is huge. Against all odds, I still love Logan. I just hated our marriage. I need to write out my thoughts in order to work through them.

I call up a new blog post and start typing away. At this point, writing the blog is almost like talking to myself, except with the identifying details obscured.

*Divorce*, I title it. There's no way anyone will know it's me, because as far as the Valley is concerned, Callie has disappeared. And there's always a high-profile divorce happening.

*I'm supposed to get half.*

I let that sentence sit there. I don't want half. Not of his money—*our* money—not the house, not his shares in Bastard Capital.

I want what I thought our marriage would be, back in the early days. Back when I thought quitting my job would be fine, that I'd find something new to do. Back when I thought Logan's work schedule would stay light, the way it was when we were dating. I could handle sixty hours a week of him being gone.

But the things I chose to fill my life with instead of a job didn't satisfy me, although they were what I was supposed to be doing. And I found that Logan being gone for over eighty hours a week was not something I could handle.

*I don't want half. I want what we had before, the promise of what our marriage should have been. Money and shares in his company don't even begin to cover the loss of that.*

The words start to flow out of me, and as the shadows grow long and Meowthra sleeps in the corner, I pour my heart out.

# CHAPTER 4

I wake up with a dry mouth and a bleary head, as if I drank myself stupid last night. I didn't touch a drop though: this is a purely Logan-induced hangover.

I push myself up against the mattress, my sheets and blankets twisted around my legs. It looks like I tried to run a marathon in bed. I don't remember my dreams, but I was clearly tossing and turning in them.

The cottage is damp and overheated, the windows coated in condensation. I closed them before I went to bed, and now it feels like the house is desperate to breathe. I crack open a few windows but leave the back door closed. I need the fresh air, but I also need to close myself in, to cover up my raw bits. I slept in my ratty old sweater, needing the comfort of it, but even tugging the sleeves over my hands isn't giving me enough protection.

Once my coffee is ready, I open my laptop. My email tells me I've had ten comments on my latest post since yesterday. Most of my commenters are regulars, and all of them comment under fake names. CoderGirl has written that I shouldn't take the shares—she knows I can make my own way. Judging by her comment history, she's one of the talented women who've been pushed aside by the Valley's dudebro culture.

KatinaKat says I should take the shares and my rightful place in the boardroom. Just elbow aside all those idiot men. My guess is that she has an MBA and is frustrated she can't use it.

The last comment makes me want to cry. Susie—no last name—comments on most of my posts. All she's said on this one is "I'm so very sorry to hear about your divorce. I wish there were some way I could help you."

I wish there were too. But I have no idea who Susie really is. My guess is that she's like me: no one who's high powered or brilliant at coding or a marketing genius. Just an ordinary woman who fell for a man who was anything but.

I close my email. The next thing I do is my own dirty secret: I pull up *TidBytes*. *TidBytes* is *the* gossip spot of Silicon Valley, part tech news and part tabloid. I hate *TidBytes*, but I can't look away from it. For the past year, it's been the very first place I've gone to on the internet, even as it makes me sick.

When the home page loads, I let myself breathe, my stomach unknotting.

Logan isn't on the front page today. He very often is though, usually with a woman in the picture. Not me—I've never been in *TidBytes*.

All the pictures of Logan—and the women with him—have been taken at parties. Things that were supposed to be business events, things he said would bore me. I believed him. At first.

But as I saw photo after photo of handsome, charming Logan with a new woman each time, the doubt slipped in. It found the crack in my heart and split it wide. It wasn't the main reason I left him, but those pictures didn't help.

Today though, it's not Logan looking back at me from the home page—it's *me*.

ARE THE BASTARDS BREAKING UP?

Oh, what a nasty clickbait headline. Of course Bastard Capital is just fine. So why do they have a photo of me?

As I read, my breathing gets faster and faster until my lungs can't keep up and I stop entirely. My hands are shaking so badly I can barely scroll through the story.

*TidBytes* knows about the divorce papers Logan handed me yesterday. Somehow they've found out. There's a very pointed mention in the story of the shares I'll be getting and how I'll be the most eligible divorcée in the Valley.

My mind gets hung up on the word *divorcée* because it's so silly and old-fashioned and looking for a scandal, when I'm not any of those things, but the distraction is better than processing the rest of the story, which is just... awful. Nauseating.

But finally my brain gets to everything *TidBytes* seems to already know about *my divorce*, and my body reacts with a bone-deep shiver. I get up and shut all the windows completely, although it's too late. Somehow, someway, this stupid gossip rag has been inside my business and seen the things only Logan and I should know.

For a brief, guilty moment, my mind flicks to the blog post I wrote yesterday. Maybe...

I snap the last window shut, cutting off the rest of that thought. If *TidBytes* knew I write *The Silicon Wife*, they'd have put me on the front page way before now. My identity isn't one of those open secrets either; people speculate on who the Silicon Wife might be right in front of me, totally oblivious. My name has never come up.

No, that secret is safe. So how did they get this info?

Maybe Logan told them. Or one of the other Bastards. That makes more sense, although it's also a stab in my gut.

To leak that before Logan even gave me the papers is pretty shitty. But they probably don't feel like they owe me anything. They never did before.

I settle back into my desk chair, having worked out some of my anxious energy. Okay, so everyone knows. They were going to know sooner or later, because I would have to sign those divorce papers. I don't want to, but accepting his entire offer is the only way Logan will let me go. If I sign, then this is over.

I reread the article—they picked a picture of me leaving a private club in San Francisco, fleeing that disastrous meeting with Mark, and thank God they didn't catch Julian in the shot too—and I have the good sense to close the browser window before I get to the comments.

Logan has to know about this. Immediately. If he didn't tell *TidBytes* about the divorce, he's going to be livid. He was always protective of my image, not letting any magazine or website get near me unless he approved. Of course, he didn't seem to care if *TidBytes* featured him all the time, but I guess that's the good old double standard at work.

I sigh and reach for my phone. I drop it at first, shocked by the coldness of it, then have to dive under the desk for it. My hair, which is way too long, flies in my face, clinging to my cheeks and catching on my lips. I shove all the strands back haphazardly because there's no one here to see me. I don't have to worry about things like that anymore.

I call up my contacts list and scroll through it. I used to call him several times a day; talking to him on the phone was sometimes the only contact I'd have with him for days. I haven't dialed him in months, but my fingers remember exactly where his info is in my phone.

There his number is, tagged with a picture of him I took with my phone. He's smiling widely, half goofy and half embarrassed, like it's awkward how happy he is with me.

It wasn't awkward to me, although it could be frightening at times, the jolt of pure pleasure that would rush through me at the sight of him. I'd see someone who looked like him on the street, and my stomach would swoop and dive.

It's diving right now, heading straight for my feet, and I'm terrified it will never settle back into place. I wrap my arm around my waist as I hit Call.

There's nothing but silence for several long seconds as the call connects. With each passing heartbeat, my stomach cramps tighter and tighter.

I pull the phone from my ear and check that I actually hit the right button. A ring comes from the tiny speaker finally.

And then a knock at the door.

This time I don't jump—only my heart does. So Logan was already on his way over. He's never been an early riser, which means he probably didn't sleep last night. He does that sometimes, paces through the night when his mind can't let go of a problem. I'd wake up in an empty bed and hear him walking in the next room. He'd try to be quiet about it, but somehow I always heard him.

I hang up before the call connects to his voice mail. My throat is dry, almost too dry to swallow past, but I do it anyway.

This is it. He's come for the signed papers. When he leaves me today, it will be for good.

Some far-off corner of my mind howls at the thought, but I shut it down before it can take over my mouth.

Instead, I open the door wide, pretending to be unafraid.

Except it's not Logan. It's a woman I've never seen before.

"Excuse me?" It's an incredibly rude way to greet someone, but it's out before I can even think.

The woman smiles, the crease of it as sharp as the ones on her trousers. She's in black from head to toe. Trousers, thin cashmere sweater, and narrow silk scarf: all identical shades of darkness.

You don't get your blacks to match that perfectly unless you put a lot of effort into it. Her hair is the only splash of color, a deep, glossy brown. Sable, like the finest paint-brushes.

"Miss Hanes? Calliope Hanes?" She holds out a hand, already expecting me to confirm it. "Minerva Dyne."

No one calls me Calliope anymore, not even my mom. I'm not sure what she was thinking when she named me that —maybe something about the Muses and the power of women, but maybe she also just thought it was pretty. Not that Mom would ever admit it.

I give Minerva Dyne's hand the briefest of squeezes, then brace myself against the door, blocking the entryway. "I'm sorry, what's this about?"

If she was expecting to be invited in, her expression doesn't show it. "I represent Corvus."

She says it like I should know what it is. "Oh. And they do?"

"Information security," she says. "Mostly."

I have no idea what that means or why it would involve me. "If you're looking for design work, I'm afraid I can't help you. I retired when I got married."

That had been an agonizing decision. Logan of course insisted I should keep my job, but my bosses got weird about my upcoming marriage. There were hints about the work my association with Logan would bring in and then outright demands that I network on behalf of the firm with all the billionaires now in my social circle.

I'm not a networker, and I thought my marriage ought to be private. Since they thought differently, I quit. I regretted it afterward when I suddenly had too much time on my hands, but I would have been in an unbearable position if I hadn't.

"I'm not here for design work." Her mouth twitches with a hint of condescending amusement. "I'm here about your marriage. Or rather, the dissolution of it."

## CHAPTER 5

"What?" I rear back so fast I'm lucky I've got a firm hold on the door. Otherwise, I might have tripped over my own feet. "How did you hear about the divorce?"

"*TidBytes*," Minerva says, as if that's where she gets all her news.

"But… but that was only posted this morning." I am very, very freaked out now. First Logan appearing yesterday, then the *TidBytes* post this morning, and now this woman appears on my doorstep. I've been hiding for so long from this world, and suddenly it's crashing back into my life like a tsunami.

"I took a helicopter up." She lifts the leather bag in her hand. "I have an offer for you. From my boss, Arne Fuchs."

*Arne Fuchs*? But I hardly know him. We've met maybe once, said hello, and that was it. I think he had dark hair? Or maybe he's going bald?

"An offer for what?" Even as I say it, I feel like an idiot. Yesterday I had nothing of value, not a single thing a tech genius could want.

Today I've potentially got shares in one of the most successful VC firms in the world.

Minerva's no dummy—she immediately catches my realization. She nods. "The Bastard Capital shares. All of them. For three hundred million."

Three hundred million is a joke, and we both know it. It's an opening offer is what it is. But she thinks enough of me that she expects me to negotiate. I don't think I've ever been taken so seriously, at least not as Logan's wife.

"I see." I lean back, make her believe I'm considering it. I don't even want the damn shares, and I certainly don't know if I'm going to sell them. Something tells me not to trust this woman with that information though. "But I don't even own the shares yet."

Fuchs must want them desperately if he's sent his assistant all the way here this quickly. He'll be only the first of the sharks looking to bite into those shares. God, I wish Logan never put them in the divorce offer. He's thinking to spare me any financial instability, but instead I'll have to deal with more offers like this.

*I don't even want the damn things*, I want to shout. *I just want to mourn my marriage in private.*

"I understand." Minerva puts so much sympathy in her voice it's unnaturally smooth. "But we'd like to arrange things quickly."

The pause before *quickly* is so small I almost imagine it.

"What if I don't want to sell the shares?"

I brace myself for the empty patter she's already prepared, nonsense about how I must want the money now, how time consuming it will be to sit on the board, how awful it will be seeing my ex-husband so often...

I mean, I was thinking along those same lines last night, trying to think how to give back the unwanted gift to Logan.

Even though I already know what she'll say, at least the outlines of it, I ask out of some instinct to stick to the script here. She's expecting me to ask, so I will.

But she doesn't react beyond blinking like I've flicked

water in her face. She opens her mouth, but nothing comes out.

*She wasn't expecting me to ask.* I've thrown her off, which throws me off. The tense set of her jaw says she's got some words she wants to say but can't let herself.

Realization prickles along my scalp. She thought I was going to say yes right away—that's why she doesn't have an answer ready. Someone told her I was more than ready to sell, that I was probably eager to sell, and I wouldn't need any convincing.

"I can't imagine you would want to keep them," she says finally. But something's off in her voice, the tone not quite matching up with the words. "Not after we come to a mutually agreeable price."

As a graphic artist, it's my job to make things people respond to on levels they can't even detect. I've gotten good at watching people as they interact with things, how text and color and design make them feel. That skill is coming in handy now.

This woman is here to sell me on something that she doesn't think I should buy.

After the weirdness of everything since yesterday, that doesn't shock me as much as it might have. There's something deeper happening here, and I don't think Logan is in on it.

Which means we'll have to talk, seriously talk, before either of us does anything.

"I don't have the shares." I keep my voice firm and chilly. "I can't discuss anything. I hope that answers *all* your questions."

She knows she's screwed up, that she's lost me, but she keeps her panic confined to the muscles around her eyes. It's impressive how well she controls her expression. "Mr. Fuchs would love to come to a deal soon so that you know your future is secure. Perhaps you might like to name your preferred asking price?"

Her voice is steady, but that last line gives away the depth of her desperation. She can't go back empty-handed.

I sympathize, because we're both caught up in something bigger than ourselves here. But I also have to turn her down.

"I can't think about anything right now beyond contacting a lawyer."

Her nose flares, and I catch my mistake—no one knew I didn't initiate the divorce. Great, that will be all over the Valley in about an hour I'm guessing.

"Are you certain? Knowing your future—"

I push the door toward her, closing it halfway. "Not today."

"My card." It snaps between her fingers as if conjured by magic. "We'll be in touch."

I take the card reluctantly, then shut the door without a farewell because I know she's telling the truth: we are definitely not finished.

Once I'm curled up on the couch, I study her card. It's incredibly simple, like something my grandfather would have carried, on matte card stock in heather gray, done in a timeless serif font. Definitely not Silicon Valley style, which goes in for logos and glossy stock on their cards—when they do cards at all.

It doesn't say what her title is at Corvus, but there is a website address. I grab my laptop and Google the company.

There are several articles about how they're helping to hunt terrorists online, keeping Americans safe, and so on. Farther down, there are some conspiracy-theory-flavored articles on lesser-known sites about how Corvus is spying on all of us through our phones. I don't know what to believe, but I suspect the truth about Corvus lies somewhere between the two extremes.

A glance at the clock tells me it's been twenty minutes since Minerva left. Plenty of time for her to get far enough away that she won't overhear.

But if Corvus is listening in through my phone, it won't matter how far away she is.

I tuck my chin deeper into my sweater cowl, shivers gusting through me. It's ridiculous to imagine a company listening in to my ordinary calls, but I can't convince myself it's not true.

I have to talk with Logan though. Privately. Which means I have to go to him.

After hiding from him for so long, I should be reluctant. Instead, my hands seem to leap toward my keys, and my legs drag me toward the door. My body is humming with eagerness at the thought of him.

I shouldn't go to him, not when just the thought of seeing him can set me off like this. But I have no choice.

Things have gotten too deep for us to swim alone.

## CHAPTER 6

"Just a minute," I say as housekeeping knocks at my room door for the second time in as many seconds.

They're damn eager to get in here, which I wouldn't have expected from such a run-down motel. But no matter how eager they are, I'm fresh out of the shower and in no state to be seen. I check the knot at my hips, making sure the towel isn't slipping, then use the other one in my hand to towel my hair one last time. Once I've got all the drips, I sling that towel over my shoulders. There. I'm covered enough to tell the housekeepers to come back later.

"Can you come—"

My voice doesn't die when I see Callie there—it's strangled in my throat.

"Logan." She's wearing the same sweater as yesterday, and her hands are knotted in the sleeves. "We have to talk."

She's so pale her complexion is ghostly. The skin around her eyes is the color of a bruise, and her hair is tangled around her shoulders.

Instantly I'm on high alert. Something's frightened her, and I'm going to find the thing and destroy it. She might not love me anymore, but I'll always defend her.

I take her arm and pull her inside, shutting the door on the outside world.

She puts a hand to her mouth, her gaze flittering and flicking over me, never landing anywhere. "You…" Her hand gestures to the towel. The lower one.

So much color floods her face then it's like watching a sunrise at high speed. Whatever's got her spooked, she's still attracted to me.

I want to pounce on that, to have her panting and needy like she used to be for me, but she's also scared.

I act like it's no big deal I'm only wearing a towel. "You've seen this before." I don't offer to put on clothes, because I'm not that much of a gentleman. "What's happened?"

She pulls out her phone like she's going to show me something, then stops. "Can they hear us? Corvus? Please tell me I'm being crazy."

Cold sparks move across my skin. "Corvus? Fucking *Fuchs* was here?"

I'm going to murder that son of a bitch. And Mark's going to be more than happy to help me. Fuchs fucked with January, the love of Mark's life, and now he's fucking with *my wife?*

I'm sure Finn knows several spots in the desert that would be perfect for a shallow grave.

Okay, so Callie doesn't want to be my wife anymore—my heart twists like it's dodging a knife—but she can't battle Fuchs on her own.

"So it's true." Callie sits on the bed with a soft moan. "Oh my God. That's how he found out."

I hate being behind in a conversation—if I'm not two steps ahead, I get surly. "Start from the beginning. But first give me your phone."

Callie isn't surprised by my tone, but that was a great thing about her—she never mistook my moods for meanness. Yes, I know I'm overbearing and too much to take, but she saw it for what it really was. And accepted me, loved me anyway.

At least she used to.

Wordlessly she hands over her phone. I pull out the battery, then set the phone and it on a side table. "Don't use that until I can fix it. You can use my phone instead. Now tell me exactly what happened."

She tears her gaze away from her phone. "You came yesterday." She tucks her hands farther into her sleeves, pulling in on herself. "With those papers."

I nod, but my neck aches as I do. "What then?"

"Last…" She shakes her head, starts over. "This morning *TidBytes* had a story on our divorce. I thought you might have told them. Or someone else."

"How the fuck did they find out?"

She flinches, and I immediately want to bite my tongue.

"I didn't tell anyone except the guys," I say more gently. "Was it someone you told?"

The shake of her head is slow and pained. "I never told anyone. I thought it was…"

"You thought one of the Bastards," I say flatly.

I've never understood it, but Callie and the rest of them have never gotten along. My parents loved her, her mom loved her, her friends loved her—so why couldn't she get along with the men who were more than brothers to me?

Her mouth compresses at my tone. "It's a reasonable conclusion."

"No, it's not." My temper surges, fed by both her assumption and Fuchs's fucking shenanigans. "They wouldn't do that."

"Whatever. That's not my main problem. Our main problem."

I fist my hands to hold in the surge of possessiveness at

that. Yes, it should always be *our*. *Our* problems. *Our* solutions.

*Get over it, idiot. Elliot was right—she just wants out.*

"What's the main problem?" I ask.

*TidBytes* knowing isn't a serious issue. Yeah, I'd like to know who leaked it, but it's not like divorces aren't public record in the end.

"So there was the story this morning." She gestures with her hand, the sleeve flapping over it. "Not five minutes after I'd read it, Minerva Dyne was on my doorstep, offering to buy my shares in Bastard Capital."

Of all the people to show up on Callie's porch... "*Minerva.*"

Callie cocks her head, watching my expression. "I see you already know her."

"Yeah. Elliot just *loves* her."

"Elliot just loves everyone," she mutters.

That's not true, but I let it slide. "Minerva is a special case. You don't know this, but we had a run-in with Fuchs and her a few weeks ago." I don't want to scare her, but I also have to let her know how serious it was. "It involved an encryption company we'd invested in. He wanted to spike their tech so he could keep spying on people through their phones."

The blood runs out of her cheeks so fast they sag. "The conspiracy nuts are right."

I raise my palms to calm her. "We handled it."

We couldn't erase all the spyware Fuchs has already gotten into people's phones, but January's program is going to stop him from using any data he manages to get. And she and Mark found each other in the process. They're so damn happy, just like Callie and I used to be, it fucking kills me.

"You don't have to worry about it."

She looks at her phone like it's turned into a snake. "It's

still creepy. Is that how he heard about…" Her tongue slips out to wet her lower lip. "The divorce."

"I don't think he did," I say. "According to what we know, the program isn't being used. My gut tells me there's a simpler explanation. But I need to confirm it."

My suspicions about *TidBytes* didn't start today. But to get at the heart of what I think's happening here, I'll need some help. So I grab my phone and call Finn.

He answers with a long, lazy "Dude. What's up?"

"Can you find out who really owns *TidBytes*? Like, immediately?"

"On it."

The line goes dead. Finn is our resident genius, the kind of guy who was hacking into the CIA before he even hit puberty. We've been tracking Fuchs's tentacles in the Valley —he's got a sucker latched on to a ton of companies—but we haven't looked into *TidBytes* yet. Some of their stories have my spider-sense tingling, like they aren't the trashy gossip blog they pretend to be but something darker. Something with an agenda behind it.

Plus they run stories on us way too much. I mean, we're some interesting fuckers but not *that* interesting.

Callie is watching me, her gaze soft but intrigued. The towel seems suddenly too tight and itchy. Fucking stupid body of mine can't focus like my mind can. Not that I ever could focus around her.

"That was Finn," I say. "He's looking into *TidBytes*. I'm guessing he'll find out that Fuchs is somehow involved with them. Which is why they ran the story—to force you to sell as soon as they made the offer."

"How would they know I'd seen it?"

"They knew you were here—" Which even I didn't know until two days ago. "*Shit*. He knew you're here."

Maybe Fuchs was tracking her phone. We were never completely certain that the program was dead.

Callie is shaking her head. "Julian knew I was here and my mom. Along with some of my friends."

Right. I knew that. I was the only one who didn't know where she was.

I run a hand through my hair and try to think, which is damn hard with Callie so near. She scrambles me.

There are a million ways Fuchs could have tracked her here, ways I didn't want to use. If Callie hadn't wanted me to know where she was, I wasn't going to go stalker on her to find her. Even though not knowing was like a cancer on my heart.

"Okay." I start to tick off on my fingers. "So Fuchs knows you're somewhere near this town. We don't know exactly how he does, but he does. He can see where people are visiting *TidBytes* from. He sees a visitor from Platina, California, pop up—I'm betting no one else here visits that site on the regular—and bam. He knows you've seen. Knows you're vulnerable. And then he swoops in."

Motherfucker. My hands flex, imagining Fuchs's throat between them. I usually go in for more modern forms of fighting—buyouts, things like that—but I can see the appeal of some old-fashioned ones right now.

"Why?" Callie asks. "Why would he want those shares so bad? He could start his own VC firm. He's rich enough."

"To fuck with us." Money isn't the point for Fuchs. He's got enough. Fucking with people in secret is how he gets his kicks. "That's why I think he owns *TidBytes*—he's putting stories in there to make us look bad."

Her mouth drops open. "Wait, those stories are planted?" She scrambles for my phone, pulls up *TidBytes*. "They're all fake?"

The hope in her voice is like a bright shard of sunlight.

Then I see the stories she's talking about. She's pulled up all the stories tagged with my name, *Logan Martell*, and is scrolling through all of them. Each one has a zoomed-in picture of me with another woman. Each and every one.

Holy fuck. How the fuck did I miss that?

Okay, so I noticed they were reporting on the parties I went to, but I never looked at the stupid-ass pictures. Never noticed before now that they were getting snaps of me with all those random women. Who the fuck wants to look at pictures of themselves in a tabloid?

But Callie navigated right to them. Callie had been seeing those pictures every time she went to the site.

"How often do you visit this site?" I ask in a hollow voice.

"Every day." The realization that I haven't said the stories were fake echoes in her words.

She saw those pictures almost every day.

And she thought I was cheating on her.

That fucking gossip rag and whoever was behind it ruined my marriage. On purpose. It wasn't *me* hurting her, being gone too much—it was Fuchs and his schemes.

"I never slept with any of those women." My jaw is tight with rage.

"I actually don't care that much even if you did." There's a hitch on *care*, because she does, her voice cracking out of its usual soft tones. "The point is, when you were out having these pictures taken, you weren't home with me."

"They were for business. I invited you, you always said no. That you hated those parties."

She turns away, her mouth set.

I put my hand under her chin and force her to look at me. "Can't you see? We've been set up. The pictures, leaking the divorce, trying to buy your shares... Fuchs is manipulating us."

I'm still pissed that she fell for it and didn't *tell* me about it and left me in agony for months but… but touching her makes me feel alive again. Painfully alive, but it's better than the numb agony of before.

Her eyes gleam with tears. "It wasn't just that."

That is not what I want to hear. But I can't let her go.

"What didn't I give you?" I ask. "If you wanted something, you only had to ask. Just tell me what to give you to make it better."

If I can convince her to come back, to make a home with me again… then maybe I can breathe again, come out of this awful nothing I am without her.

"I only ever wanted you." That's lower than a whisper.

"You always had me." How did she not understand that? Yeah, there were those shitty pictures, but I came home every night to her. Home to a house I built just for her, filled with things I bought to please her.

She opens her mouth, ready to protest. So to prove it to her, I capture her mouth with mine.

## CHAPTER 7

For the first time in forever, I'm not thinking.

There's Logan's mouth on mine, his hands on my torso, his hips pressed hard against my pelvis, and my body takes command. I can't worry or fret or even imagine beyond this moment, because all I can do is feel.

His kiss is hungry and soul deep, and my heart unfurls under it like one of the roses I keep trying to paint. I put my hands to his jaw, the razor-sharp line of it that makes his face so unforgettable. There's stubble there and warm skin, and I swear I feel his pulse beneath my palms.

I kiss him back, half desperate, half longing, because it's been forever since I've touched him and my skin misses him. The way Logan touches me—no one ever touched me like that, not before or since, and my body craves it.

He slips a hand under my sweater, his palm finding the bare skin of my stomach. I gasp, because it's like being shocked back alive.

*This* is what it feels like to be touched. *This* is what it feels like to be desired. *This* is what it feels like to be truly alive.

Logan groans, a vibration of painful pleasure that echoes through both of us. Our mouths are fused together, and I don't think either of us could break free if our lives depended on it.

His hand makes his way up my torso, his fingers marking off my ribs, claiming that territory as his own once more. I'm not wearing a bra—I hardly ever do—and my breasts tighten in anticipation, my nipples hardening. I have to pull my mouth away from his to gasp.

"Do you remember now?" His whisper in my ear is a rough rasp. "How we are together? The way I make you feel?" His hips thrust against mine. "How I make you feel?"

I *had* forgotten. The memories were there, in dreams, and in my waking moments I told myself I was only lonely, that my body couldn't crave him that much.

But it does.

He kisses his way along my jaw. I tilt my head back, completely surrendering to him. It's like being offered water after crossing Death Valley—you could tell me it's poisoned, and I'd still take it.

"Let me love you again," he says.

I jump like I've been stung. Somehow the word *love* gets through to me, shocks my brain into taking back control.

"No." I try to put a hand between us, but Logan isn't giving up even a millimeter. "I didn't come here for this."

He's not exactly fighting me, but he's also not letting go. His expression is tight with suppressed anger.

I shift again, trying to break out of his arms... and my hand catches on his towel. Before I can stop it, it comes loose and falls to the floor.

I go very, very still. I keep my eyes hard on the dingy carpet, as if even catching a glimpse of his nakedness will strike me blind.

"Looks like we have a situation here." His voice rumbles through me.

He releases me, then takes a step back. I'm still staring at the carpet as though my life depends on it, but in the corner of my eye, I see his hands lift.

He's backing away from me with his arms raised as if I'm the dangerous one.

"Could you please put back on the towel?" I say, my voice thin with embarrassment. And frustrated desire.

"You pulled it off."

"That's—" I snap my gaze to him without thinking and immediately regret it.

He's even more beautiful naked, his body as classically handsome as his face. My mouth goes dry, and my sexual frustration turns all the way up to eleven.

"*Please*," I say through a clenched jaw. I grab the towel from the floor and toss it at him, my hands shaking as I do.

Somehow, through an insane force of will, I manage to look back at the carpet, which looks even dingier than before. Compared to Logan's skin, everything looks pathetic though.

"It's safe now," he says dryly.

It isn't, because it won't be safe until he's back in the City and I'm back in my cottage. But then there are still the divorce papers waiting for me at home…

His phone rings, interrupting my thoughts. He grabs it from the nightstand before it has a chance to ring a second time.

"Yeah?" he says.

Logan glances over his shoulder at me, the muscles in his back rippling. He always keeps himself in excellent shape, approaching his workouts with an intensity an Olympian would envy. When he's sweating, shaking, with nothing left to give—that's when he considers a workout done. I loved catching him after, because he always found that last extra ten percent within to fuck me against whatever was handy. I'd lick the sweat off him, salt and musk and effort, while he'd bring me to a screaming climax.

"Son of a bitch," he mutters into the phone. "We should have checked from the very beginning."

He looks back at me as if reassuring himself I'm still here, torn between watching me and trying to make his conversation semiprivate.

I put my hand to his shoulder and pull. He turns to me, smooth and controlled, because he won't let his body be anything but a precision instrument.

I won't let him make this conversation private because this situation involves the both of us. And we are still married.

If Logan can't turn to me now, then I might as well sign the papers and leave.

His hand finds my upper arm, lightly at first, unsure of his welcome. I don't push it away, but I don't lean into his touch either. I'm shocked into stillness, to be honest, because this is way more intimate than sex, which is crazy.

But this is what we used to do, back when we were happy. Share simple things, like a work call. Like a touch.

"Shut up," he growls at the phone.

I jump, although he's not talking to me. I've forgotten how the Bastards talk to each other—insults that would make my hair curl, they toss out with affection. That kind of rough-and-tumble, I-can't-show-you-how-much-I-care male affection has always been odd to me.

"I should have fucking well known," he goes on. "Look at all the bullshit they print about me. Something was up."

*Is it Finn?* I mouth to him.

Logan opens his mouth to answer, then interrupts whoever's on the phone again. "They went after Callie."

His hand tightens on my arm, and his gaze flicks to mine.

There's a promise there, deep and sure. He's going to protect me, no matter what. Even if I don't want him to.

"Since they did that," he says, "I want to bury them. Sue them out of existence."

My nape prickles. Logan's always been ready to protect me, but this… He sounds like a bad movie script. It feels wrong from him. He's not a "Hulk smash" kind of guy. Subtlety is more his style, even when it comes to ruining someone.

"I don't care how long it takes, Elliot—"

Oh great, it's Elliot, not Finn. And he's talking Logan out of suing? Isn't suing people what lawyers do for fun on Friday nights?

I pull my arm out of Logan's grasp and gesture at the phone. "Can we discuss this before you start a lawsuit?"

Logan cups his hand over the end of the phone. "I can put it on speaker."

Right, so I'll have to deal with him and Elliot at the same time. Anything I say, Elliot is sure to shoot down with his logic missiles.

"No." I reach for the phone. "I want to discuss it with you, not you and your brother. I'm not married to him."

There's a flicker in Logan's gaze. He's either pleased or shocked I've brought that up. Maybe both.

Without breaking eye contact with me, he says, "Elliot, I'll have to call you back."

He hangs up but not before I hear Elliot's angry yelp. I can't help my smile.

"Okay." Logan sets the phone aside. "Let's talk. But if you're thinking I'm going to let this slide, not when you ran away from me because of it—"

I put a finger to his lips. God, after not touching him for so long, to have that freedom again is like a drug. And taking that freedom is also a bad idea, just like taking drugs.

"*TidBytes* didn't make me run." I keep saying it to him, and I hope this time it finally sinks in.

"The hell it didn't. Seeing those pictures every day must have hurt. Must have destroyed your trust in me."

I can't deny that they did hurt. And that, yes, it was harder to trust him. But we'd been pulling away from each other before that.

"Okay, so they didn't help." I can admit to that. "But you were never home. I gave up my job, my career, to sit at home waiting for you, and you were never there!"

He stares for a long moment. Never before have I spoken to him with such rage, such venom. "I never asked you to do those things. Callie, if you wanted a job, you could have had one. I'm not some caveman."

I roll my eyes because I have no idea how to make him understand. "I went into this marriage thinking you wanted a partner. But in the end, I was only a wife."

The moment I say *wife*, my eyes widen and I clap my hand over my mouth.

*I* said those words, but they were my mother's before this. That phrase popped out of me because I've heard her use it so many times.

I've never met my father. At least I don't remember him. And not because my mother used him like a sperm donor— no, they were married. I came along twelve months after they did, so it wasn't even necessary for them to get hitched.

I have to assume they married because they loved each other. Why else would my mother have done that?

But when I was two, my mother left him and never looked back. She didn't hide that from me, and she wasn't resentful of my dad and the fact that he wasn't around. She never really talked about what it was like when they were together though, only how she left in the end.

When I asked her about him—why my mother married

him, why she left, she said with perfect honesty: "I thought he wanted a partner. But it turned out all he wanted was a wife. And that's not who I am."

She warned me of that exact same thing when I told her I was marrying Logan. And I told her that Logan was wealthy enough that he didn't need a wife. He didn't need someone to cook or clean or watch his kids or even to keep his bed warm—so if he married me, it was because he *wanted* me.

Not every relationship has to be some patriarchal power struggle, and I was going to show her that mine definitely wasn't. That love could win.

Somewhere around the fiftieth picture of Logan on *TidBytes*, as I got ready for yet another charity board meeting that didn't really need me, I realized my mother was right all along. And that I needed to get out.

I have no idea how to explain that to Logan though. He's never appreciated my mom.

Logan is furious now, but he's holding it back, his nostrils flaring with the effort. "Only a wife? I don't want a wife. I wanted you."

"Then why weren't you ever there for me?"

"I was!"

"No, you weren't. The numbers don't lie. Those eighty-hour weeks away didn't lie. And pictures don't either. Otherwise, how could *TidBytes* have all those pictures of you to publish?"

"It was work!" He roars that, as if by pure volume he can make me accept his argument.

"Right." I cross my arms and suddenly realize that we're fighting in a crappy hotel room. But it's too late to stop now. "It *was* work. Always. All the time."

"I can't..."

Logan doesn't finish, but I already know what he can't do

—slow down. Even now, he's pacing like a caged wolf, rangy energy animating him.

I dip my head and sigh. "You think it's just that simple," I say, "that while you're working eighty-hour weeks, I'll find something to do and be waiting and ready whenever you come back."

Suddenly he stops, shakes his head. "We're not doing this again. Can't you see this is exactly what Fuchs wants? A wedge between us?"

He's still not seeing what I mean. "I don't know Arne Fuchs at all. He has nothing to do with this."

"But he does." Logan starts pacing again. "Imagine if you never saw those pictures, never had them shoved in your face every morning. Imagine where our marriage might be if you'd talked to me, trusted in me."

It would look the same. Him never around, me rattling around in a role I couldn't be happy in...

But those pictures did worm their way into my brain, whispering evil thoughts to me. Why else would I look at *TidBytes* every damn day if it wasn't getting inside my head, exactly like Logan claims Fuchs wanted?

I put a fist to my forehead to stop the spinning behind my eyes. *I just don't know.* I knew within a month of being with him that I wanted to marry Logan. But I don't know if I want to end this.

I let my fist drop, rub my hand over my mouth. I have to tell him everything. It's bubbling inside me like hot-spring mud.

"I thought I was pregnant."

Logan looks as sick as I feel, his limbs slowing like time is stopping. "What happened? Did you... Have you seen a doctor?"

I shake my head. "I was late, that's all. About a week. I thought I'd tell you, and we could take the test together, and… I let myself get excited. About everything it might mean."

I was happy, thrilled, things I hadn't been in a long, long time. I had hope, another thing that had been in short supply.

Then it was all gone, and I couldn't keep living like that.

"Why didn't you tell me?"

"I didn't see you for five days straight." My eyes sting, and I rub away the tears. "Do you remember?"

I did. I had this wonderful, beautiful thing to share with him, a renewal of all our hopes… and he left me completely alone with it.

"The launch for that GPS app was fucked up." He tugs at his hair, and I can't tell if he's upset about my not telling him or about the launch going wrong. "I slept in my office all those nights."

"I was getting ready to call you. I figured…" I shrug, because whatever I was thinking then—about how he was busy, how I shouldn't disturb him—seems so unimportant now. "That morning I was ready to call you. And then my period started. I was crying, realizing that everything I'd imagined wasn't going to happen." I take a shaky breath. "And there was another picture of you on the front page of *TidBytes*. I was waiting for you so long, and there you were, so far away from me."

I look away, because it's easier than looking at him and remembering how badly he'd let me down.

"There was?" he asks. The confusion in his voice is large and genuine. "But I was working. I swear."

"I know that. It was an old picture they put on a story about the GPS app launch. But it still hurt like all hell. And I knew I had to get out. I couldn't breathe anymore."

I can't breathe now. Maybe that's my answer. I can't breathe without him and I can't breathe with him. Yes, these months apart haven't been good—numbness is never good—but it's better than slowly suffocating to death.

"Callie." Logan's close enough to make my hair stir with his breath. "I'm so, so sorry. I had no idea about any of this."

My entire body wants to turn to him, tuck myself into the curve of him. I hold very, very still instead. Because he's not sorry he wasn't there for me—he's sorry because he didn't know. Which is a very different thing.

"I'm okay now," I say, which isn't entirely a lie. I've accepted that there won't be a baby and that the hope I had for our marriage was an illusion. It doesn't feel good to accept those things, but the truth hurts sometimes.

He threads his fingers through mine and holds on tight. "After everything you've told me, all the things with *TidBytes*, we need to—"

"Don't ask me to try again." My fingers clench instinctively on his. "Fuchs didn't make you sleep in your office that week. Or any of the weeks before."

There's a long beat of silence, and I'm certain we're thinking the same thing. No, it wasn't Fuchs who made Logan do that—it was Logan's own innate nature that did, his unholy drive.

He brings my hand to his lips, kisses my fingers softly. "I wish I had known," he says. "I wish I'd been there for you. And I wish you'd told me. I was only ever just a phone call away."

He was, but he also wasn't. "It's over now," I say. There's no point wishing things could have gone differently, because they didn't.

"It's not over," he says. "Not with Fuchs targeting you. Hell, he targeted both of us, hurt both of us with his bullshit gossip site. We both need to take it down."

I definitely don't want *TidBytes* to target some other poor couple, but corporate power plays are his style, not mine.

"You don't need me to sue it out of existence. You've got Elliot for that." I practically spit out that last sentence.

His brow crinkles. "You make that sound bad."

"It seems... underhanded." I shrug. "Not like you. You don't fight in a courtroom, you fight out in the real world. Remember when that patent troll moved in on you?"

He smiles. "Yeah. Instead of paying him off, I invented something that did the job better. And he didn't get a penny."

Electricity crackles down my neck, lights up my spine. "Wait." I shake my finger at him, thoughts jostling through my mind. "You invented something better."

Ideas are zapping through my brain, and I can already see the outlines of a logo—bold but also inviting. *Come in and chat, share the news*, it says.

*Bigger and better than TidBytes*, it says. I release a low exhale as the image coalesces into something more than a notion. Something that we could actually build. Together.

"Callie?" Worry vibrates through Logan's voice.

"We don't sue him," I say. "We invent something better." Of course—exactly what Logan did before. My hand tightens on his. "I'm saying that we build our own tech news and gossip site and outcompete him."

## CHAPTER 8

Logan

Callie's so damn animated, with her eyes flashing and her cheeks flushed, I want to eat her up. I haven't seen her like this in forever, and it's like finding a roaring fire after being stuck in an eternal blizzard. I *need* that expression of hers, if only to make all the work I do worth it.

But a *gossip site*? "I can't build a news site. I have no idea how to."

"How did *TidBytes* do it? We're not engineering a rocket here."

A rocket would be easier: I understand the general principles there. A gossip site means getting people to talk to you, tell you their deepest secrets.

I've fucking failed at that with my own damn wife—how will I do it with strangers?

But she loves the idea. She's gone from shattered and crying and confessing to excited and enthused all in the space of a few minutes, thanks to her idea. I mean, it's a crazy idea—what the hell do either of us know about media companies?—but it's *hers*.

And she keeps saying *we.* I'd do just about anything to

keep her saying that. Which means I have to do something to make this website happen.

"We'll hire some people," I say. "Give them the funding. Back in the office we've probably got a hundred prospectuses from people wanting to start a news site."

She shakes her head, her long hair sliding across her shoulders. "No, we can't hand this off. It has to be us managing it if it's going to mean a real victory against this guy."

That makes a... certain sense. I'd like to personally shove Fuchs's face into a wall rather than hiring someone to do it, but Callie's not vicious like me. She's supposed to be the nice one.

It seems I've underestimated her appetite for revenge.

But that doesn't change one simple fact: "I'm just not the person to do it."

"You are. We are." She's believing that so hard I'm almost convinced. "You've got contacts with all the CEOs and VCs in the Valley, and I know all their wives. Plus aren't journalists getting laid off left and right? I bet we could find a ton of talented writers dying to write about the Valley the way *TidBytes* does."

I can't refute any of that. "We'll make enemies if we do this."

There're a ~~lot~~ of people in the tech world who think the press has no business reporting on us, at least about the things we don't approve of, like personal lives, product failures, or dropping stock prices.

She makes a dismissive noise. "So does *TidBytes*. I bet we're not the first people they've targeted. I bet there're a lot of techies out there who'd love some revenge."

She's right about all that. Every one of the Bastards would be happy to see *TidBytes* go down, and I can think of at least three CEOs who are pissed about their coverage on the site. Ultrapowerful CEOs.

If we launch a site that eclipses *TidBytes*, Fuchs will explode. He's amazingly thin-skinned. It would mess with his head much worse than simply shutting *TidBytes* down.

And if we started spreading around that he was the one backing the site…

I fold my arms and lean back against the wall. Yeah, we could do a lot of damage to Fuchs here beyond just suing him. "I guess it makes sense."

Callie giggles.

"What?" I ask.

She folds her arms in imitation of me. "You've put on your corporate face. But you're wearing a towel in a crappy hotel room. It's just cu—" She swallows the rest of that, hard. "Funny. You look funny."

Callie is the only person to ever call me cute. Not even my mom did that; she was too busy keeping us clothed and fed since my dad couldn't contribute shit.

Cute was on Callie's lips all the time, or at least it used to be. The way I ate chips was cute, the way I read a book was cute, the way I cussed out other drivers under my breath was cute.

I didn't feel cute, but I did feel loved.

"We could adjourn to the business center." My voice is too serious, but I can't help it. I can only hope she sees the joke and keeps laughing.

"This place doesn't have one. It's not a motel for that kind of business."

No, it's for tourists and trysts, this place. My pulse leaps at the way her gaze cuts to the bed, shy but remembering.

It hits me then how I can turn this to my advantage. I still want her even though she left me. And now that *TidBytes* isn't fucking with her head, she'll see how ridiculous it was to run from the life we had.

She wants this website to take down *TidBytes*. And I want her.

Callie doesn't realize it, but we're negotiating here. I really have put on my corporate face.

"So we *are* doing business then," I drawl.

Her gaze cuts to mine, wide and startled. "Business?"

"You want something from me." I roll my shoulders. "And I want something from you."

I hold her gaze, never letting go, impressing on her how dead serious I am.

She puts a hand to her throat, finding the high neck of that ugly sweater she's wearing. I can't see it, but I'm guessing her pulse is going a mile a minute.

Excellent.

"You're negotiating with me?" Her voice is faint. "You've never talked like that before."

"Not to you." I lean forward, coming into her space. "But it thrilled you, didn't it? My being the hard-assed businessman."

She doesn't deny it. Instead, a hint of pink spreads through her cheeks. "What do you want from me?"

I laugh softly. Sweet, innocent Callie. "I think you know what I want."

What I'm doing is beyond the edge of morality, manipulating my wife like this. But this is also who she married—I'm a Bastard, and I'm the biggest bastard of all when I'm going after something I want.

"You'll have to say it." Her mouth purses defiantly. "If we're negotiating."

"I want you to try again." I don't even flinch as I say that, although my gut clenches. I might be playing the cold asshole, but I'm also intensely vulnerable, the way I always am with her. "Come home, to our house. Be my wife again."

Her hands uncurl inside the sleeves of her sweater, and then she pushes them out past her cuffs, exposing them. "For how long?"

Oh, she thinks she's being coy, but I know I've got her. If she was that committed to ending our marriage, she would have said no outright, not continued the negotiation. I suppress my smile through well-honed practice.

When she's back in the City, back among the life I built for her, without Fuchs pouring poison into her ear, she'll see she was wrong. Wrong to leave me, wrong to give up on our marriage.

Whatever time period I give her now won't matter, because once she's back in my bed, she's not going anywhere.

"Until the website is launched." That will take several months, at least. "After that, I'll give you whatever terms in the divorce you want."

"No shares in the Bastards," she immediately says. "I never wanted those, and I don't want to deal with them."

"Fine." I'm lying, but she'll never have the chance to find that out. I hold out my hand. "Do we have a deal?"

She pulls her lush lower lip into her mouth, worries it with her teeth. I pray that the towel is thick enough to hide my reaction.

"And sex?" she asks. She looks torn between hope and despair.

"Sleeping together is what married people do. If you can't commit fully to trying again…" I spread my hands wide, my signal that I'll walk away, no sweat.

It's another lie though.

Her hands disappear into her sleeves again, the fabric drawing tight over her fists. She's not used to this—she has no quick parry ready to go.

Holy hell, but I'm an asshole. Some dim portion of my brain is screaming at me, telling me she'll never forgive me for this.

The louder portion is screaming, *Fuck it, take what's yours. And she is yours.*

"I don't want to get pregnant again," she finally says. But the despair hasn't won out in her expression, not yet.

It's won the battle in my gut though, knocking the breath clear out of me. I can't let on though, can't give up my advantage now. I'm too close to getting her back where she belongs.

"You weren't pregnant before," I say, keeping my voice cool and steady. "And any child of ours would have the world at their fingertips."

She closes her eyes for a moment, and I almost, almost break. Almost tell her to forget it, that she can have her website, her divorce, and anything else she wants. I'll never bother her again.

But if I do that, I'll have nothing left. Nothing except work. And what is work without her?

So I keep my mouth shut and my expression hard.

"Well?" I prompt her.

She ignores my outstretched hand. "I agree." Her chest rises as she fills her lungs, and her expression crystallizes into resolve. "To try again."

I don't feel as triumphant as I ought to. Probably because her expression promises that she'll extract some concessions from me before all this is over.

## CHAPTER 9

We arrive back in the City in record time.

Logan drives like he does everything else: hard and fast and totally intent on what he's doing. Even though he's pushing the car to speeds I wouldn't dare try on my own, I'm not worried. At least not about his driving.

I am worried about what I've agreed to. Yes, I want to stop Fuchs, because what he did to us was really rotten. But my coming back doesn't mean our marriage is magically fixed. Logan is still going to work too much, and I'll still feel completely lost in his world. If we go on the way we have been.

It's the chance that it might not, sliver thin as it is, that has me in this car, riding next to him, going back to our life. When I ran, I didn't want to admit my marriage might be over. And I still don't want to admit that. I still want to fight for it.

Logan in full Bastard mode, negotiating with me like he was going to take everything he could and never feel a flicker of hesitation... it was hot. Superhot. My mother would be appalled, but it turns out I like the caveman act.

When we zip down the 80 past Berkeley and then hit the usual traffic jam just before the Bay Bridge, I crane forward in my seat, taking in the view of San Francisco from across the water. It really is a gorgeous city, and seeing it again makes me realize how much I've missed it.

I point out the window. "Look, Meowthra. There's your new home."

From the back seat, Meowthra yawns and then returns to licking his paws. He's as unexcited as I was anxious.

Logan took over the moment I said I'd return with him. Calls were made, and my house would be packed up, my car driven back to the City, and my lease dealt with, all by someone other than me. I wouldn't have to lift a finger.

We did go back to my cottage for a few things I'd need, and as I was putting my art supplies in the back seat—I'd already filled the trunk—Meowthra hopped in. And wouldn't be budged. I frantically called the owner, explaining that I might be kidnapping his cat against my will, but he only laughed and said, "I told you he goes where he wants. Looks like he wants to go with you."

So here I was, returning to the city I loved with an estranged husband and a semiferal cat. An odd way to cross the Bay Bridge, but San Francisco has seen weirder. That's what I love about it.

But then Logan goes past the Bay Bridge, cutting over to the 880. My fists tighten in my lap, and I have to press my lips hard together when I realize where we're actually going.

Of course we can't go straight home. We just *have* to stop by the office, which is more like Logan's home, given how much time he spends there. The 880 will take us along the bay to South Bay, past the City entirely, and we'll loop around the base of the bay up to Palo Alto and the offices of Bastard Capital.

I keep quiet the entire ride, not that I've been talking

much. But I don't even look out the windows anymore, at the bay going by or the salt ponds there. I'm too anxious about what's going to happen when we arrive.

Logan doesn't say anything either, not even as we pull into his reserved parking spot, right next to the other Bastards' Teslas. I can't tell if it's because he's concentrating on his driving or if he's anxious too.

Bastard Capital is pretty blah from the outside, just like every other VC firm on Sand Hill Road. My logo sits discreetly next to the front door. They wanted something very old-school, clubby, yet also amused. Sort of a wink— *yeah, we know what we're expected to do, but don't expect us to do it.*

Bastard turned out to be a surprisingly easy word to make elegant. It's the two a's in it, which stand out in more traditional fonts. Even though my marriage didn't work out, I'm still proud of this logo.

This office is where Logan and I first met, together poring over logos and color palettes and branding options. He invited me out that first day, but I told him I couldn't date clients. I wanted so badly to say yes. Clients had hit on me before—God, it sometimes seemed like clients did nothing but—but it was easy saying no to them.

It was almost impossible to say no to Logan though, although I somehow managed it. The day I handed in my finished work and my firm announced I was done, he asked me out again. That time I said yes.

A date was almost beside the point by then. We'd spent so much time together on the designs I was already half in love with him. Three months later, he proposed. I didn't hesitate to say yes.

Maybe I should have.

Logan takes my hand as he leads me inside. I should pull

it away, walk in on my own two feet, but I also want his protection against his adopted brothers.

*See? He wants to be with me. I'm not stealing him from you.* Which is very teenager-like of me, but I'm so keyed up and mixed up I do feel like a teenager again. Gawky and gangly and out of place.

Their receptionist is a young man who looks awestruck at the sight of Logan. I don't remember him, so they must have hired someone new recently. "How are you, Mr. Martell?" His stance is as stiff and painful as a raw recruit's.

"Good." Although Logan's voice is too harsh for him to actually be *good.* Logan hands over Meowthra to the receptionist, who takes him with only a flicker of surprise. "Is Mark here?"

"I'm sorry, everyone except Mr. Martell—your brother— is gone for the DataHub meeting. I don't expect them back for several hours." His gaze cuts furtively to me, then to my hand clasped in Logan's. His eyes widen in a way that tells me he knows exactly who I am and why Logan holding my hand is so shocking.

I swallow hard, my fingers twitching.

Logan doesn't seem to notice. "Shit," he says at that news. "That means Anjie's gone too."

My heart sinks. Anjie was one of my few friends at Bastard Capital. It would have been nice to see her today. Instead, I'm getting Elliot.

Logan pulls me forward. "I'll go find my brother," he tells the receptionist. "We're not to be disturbed."

As we move through the curving halls—the office is designed to flow like water—junior associates stare from behind their laptop screens, some discreetly, some openly. Logan and I are the soap opera of the century around here, starring the too handsome, insanely rich bad boy of tech and the wife who was crazy enough to leave him.

Right before their very eyes, the bad boy is dragging his missing wife through the office to the firm's lawyer. I'm sure they're all anticipating something very juicy is about to happen right here.

I don't make eye contact with any of them, keeping my head high and my gaze aimed over Logan's shoulder. I can see them from my peripheral vision, and that's more than enough for me.

Logan doesn't knock when he comes to Elliot's door, he simply throws it open.

"We've got problems," he starts off.

Elliot is behind his desk, marking something with a red pen. He looks exactly the same: three-piece gray tweed suit, wire-rimmed glasses, and stern expression. I'd accuse him of being a hipster given how he dresses, but Elliot is too tight-assed to know what a hipster is.

When Elliot catches sight of me, his expression hardens like permafrost. I stare back, trying not to shiver.

"If there's something wrong with the divorce settlement…" He lets that hang like a noose.

I don't let myself react, because I know that's what Elliot wants. But inside, I'm shuddering, wishing I could pull myself into my sweater like a turtle into its shell.

"We're not signing that." Logan tosses himself into one of the chairs. "We've got to do something about *TidBytes*."

Elliot shifts, his gaze cutting from Logan to me and then back again. "After looking over the posts in question, I don't know that we have a strong case for libel. But even a suit we can't win sends a strong message that we won't tolerate any more stories." His jaw tightens. "And why aren't you signing the divorce agreement?"

"It's not because I want more." My words are as cold as his tone.

Logan shakes his head. "You two need to stop snarling at each other. Callie, sit down."

I tuck my hands into my sweater sleeves before I do. Being confronted with Elliot the very first time I step back into this place is doing a number on my stomach.

"What exactly are we doing here?" I ask Logan. "Is he a web designer now?"

Elliot's confused frown gives me a burst of mean pleasure. He's always so smug; it's nice to be ahead of him for once.

Logan doesn't answer me, at least not directly. "We'll need to set up a corporation. A media company along with all the bank accounts and such. Say five million to start with, just so we can get some people hired."

"A media company?" Elliot asks. I didn't know he could lift his eyebrows that high. "What the hell do we need a media company for?"

"We're going to beat Fuchs at his own game." Logan sends me a dazzling smile. "Oh. I forgot. Hand me your phone."

The sudden change in subject has me spluttering. "My phone?"

Okay, so he is my husband—*estranged* husband—and we're reconciling, but it's my *phone.* I feel like he's asking me to hand over my underwear.

"Yep." He holds out his hand, palm up.

"What are you going to do with it?"

"Give it to January to make it Fuchs-proof."

That doesn't make sense to me, but I've never been a computer person. I mean, I used to use them every day for my design work, but that doesn't mean I understand them any more than flipping a light switch every day makes me an electrical engineer.

When I hand the phone over, Logan tosses it immediately to Elliot, who catches it with one hand, his expression sour.

"See that January gets that," Logan says.

"I haven't even met this January," I protest weakly. "What is she going to do with it?"

"Don't worry about that." Logan's tone manages to be both bright and condescending all at once. And okay, maybe I wouldn't understand, but I'm tired, confused, and upset, and he's just taken my phone.

Elliot sets my phone down, distaste on his face. "I'll contact her and see what she can do. Now, what was this about a media company?"

Logan looks at me and waits. "Go on. It was your idea."

Suddenly, with Elliot's cold eyes staring at me, it seems incredibly silly. Elliot wants to simply sue Fuchs, and here in his office, surrounded by all the markers of his lawyerly expertise, it seems crazy to contradict him.

But I'm a designer, and I know why he's got the law books and the briefs out and the red pen—Elliot's made himself a place where he's the expert and not to be questioned. I'm being manipulated by the set he's built here.

"We're going to make our own news site. Better than *TidBytes*, and we'll take their audience away." I straighten my shoulders once I'm done, even though I should have done it before I started talking.

Elliot stares for a moment, his expression stony, and then he pops his jaw as his gaze slides over to Logan.

Logan's looking at me, not quite smiling but with clear warmth in his expression. Somehow between when I walked into his motel room and now, I've convinced him this really is a good idea.

"Callie, could we have a moment?" Elliot finally asks, still watching his brother.

I want to say no, that I have a right to be here... but I'm not sure that I do. I left Logan, and I don't know where our marriage is now. It's not fixed, that's for sure.

I might not be Logan's wife in the future, but Elliot will always be his brother.

"Sure." My voice quivers, but it's so small I don't think they hear it. At least I hope they didn't hear it. "I'll just grab the cat and wait in the car."

Logan doesn't say anything, so I take that as my cue to leave.

## CHAPTER 10

"What the hell is going on?" Elliot demands the second Callie shuts the door behind her.

I knew this was coming, only I expected all the Bastards to be here and to get a full interrogation. But Elliot alone will be tough enough—he's been pushing for me to start divorce proceedings for a while.

"I told you, we're starting a media company." I shift in the chair, crossing one leg over my knee. "You still know how to file the LLC paperwork, right?"

"My paralegal—" Elliot closes his eyes, and I swear I can hear his teeth grinding. He hates being derailed. "I don't mean the media company. I mean Callie. And you. You leave with divorce papers, then come back with her and some crazy scheme."

I tap my fingers against my leg, trying to hold in my temper. I love my little brother, but my marriage is my own business. And it's not crazy—it's my chance to win back my wife even if I had to manipulate her into it.

Not that Elliot would get that. I've always tried to keep her interactions with Elliot and the other guys to a minimum because she's clearly not comfortable with them. Which is fine. I mean, I'd like her to be close with them, but she doesn't really fit into the high-T atmosphere around here.

Elliot doesn't understand that though. He doesn't make compromises for anyone, much less romantic partners. It's why he's perennially single.

"We talked about the divorce settlement." I shrug, although my shoulders are tight. "When she realized *TidBytes* was behind it all, she agreed to come back."

Okay, I'm lying here—a little bit—but that's the truth that matters. Callie is confused at the moment, having been away too long. Now that we're back together, she'll see that her life with me is too good to leave again.

And maybe I can cut back on work. A little bit. Just enough to ease her mind. I owe her that much after not being there during her pregnancy scare.

Elliot taps his pen furiously against his desk, the only sign he's about to explode. "She left just because of some pictures on a blog?"

"Yep." I loop my arm over the back of my chair, daring him to contradict me.

Elliot drops the pen to his desk blotter—he's so fucking old-fashioned—then picks it up and puts it in the cup next to his desk clock. "Okay. Fine." His words are as sharp and precise as his movements. "I'll just put the divorce filings on hold then. And"—again, I can almost hear his teeth grinding —"start a new LLC. For a *media company.*"

Elliot still isn't seeing it, but he will once I've explained it all. "Remember when Fuchs came after January?" I ask.

"Of course."

I uncross my legs and lean in. "Fuchs plays dirty. Yeah, I'd love to sue him into nothingness, but face it, that won't work. We sue and he just takes down the pictures and writes off the legal fees, which are pocket change to him. Then *TidBytes* goes on with their fucking rumor campaigns we can't fight, and then what?"

Elliot's wearing his you're-right-and-that-pisses-me-off face. "I'll admit that makes a certain kind of sense."

I roll my eyes. For all his insistence on logic and reason, Elliot can argue any side of a position and often does just to be contrary. I sense him winding up to do that right now.

Elliot stabs a finger at me. "But you don't know anything about blogs." His finger swings to the closed office door. "And neither does she."

"We'll hire people."

His breath hisses out like steam from a geyser. He works his jaw and looks up toward the ceiling. "I think... I think maybe seeing Callie again has—"

"Stop." My tone is cold, colder than I've been with him since we were kids. "You're my brother and I love you... but she's my wife."

Elliot isn't fazed. "She left you. Jesus, Logan, you were a fucking wreck!"

My skin goes tight and cold as I remember those long months without her. He's right. They all tried to snap me out of it—more projects to manage, birthdays on Alcatraz, introducing me to every single woman they knew—but nothing worked.

Nothing but seeing Callie again.

Now that I have her back, I'm never letting her go again.

"The *TidBytes* stuff fucked with her head," I say, more casual than I feel. "Now that she's back, things will be fine. She wants to do this website thing—fine, I'll give her a website. If it means fucking up Fuchs's schemes too, awesome." I set my palm on the desk and press, the closest I'll come to begging him. "So do the LLC stuff. Please."

"I don't know if you actually believe what you're saying."

Elliot steeples his fingers, pulls a harsh breath in. "I don't want to see you hurt again."

*Hell.* That's the problem with arguing with your brother —he can pull out emotional gut punches like this.

I stand up and reach across the desk to clasp his shoulder. "Everything will be fine this time, baby bro. I'll make sure of it."

His expression goes sour because he hates being called a baby or bro. "All right. If you say so."

I settle back in the chair, confident he's done with the mushy stuff. "The hard part was convincing her to come back. Now that's done, it's easy from here."

Elliot shakes his head. He's not convinced, but he'll let the argument slide. He probably thinks he secretly won it or something. "Fine. I'll do the LLC. But remember, suing remains an option."

"I'll keep that in mind," I say dryly, because Elliot will probably remind me of it every damn day. I snap my fingers, remembering. "Oh, and you'll love this—Minerva Dyne came herself to convince Callie to sell the shares."

Elliot's stance tightens like a big cat smelling blood. "She did? What did she say?"

"I wasn't there, but from what Callie said, Minerva tried to make it sound like they were doing her a favor taking the shares off her hands."

If I had been there, Minerva would have had an earful to carry back to her boss. As it is, I'll have to call Fuchs for a little chat. Explain to him what's going to happen if he or one of his lackeys come within fifty feet of my wife ever again.

"Motherfucker." Elliot hisses. "I can't believe that bastard was listening on her phone."

My stomach swoops, but I hold my expression still. "Maybe he was, maybe he wasn't." There are other explanations for how Fuchs found her; fixing her phone isn't going to be enough to keep her safe. "Somehow he already knew where she was. If he had someone watching her, as soon as I showed up, then left all pissed off, they guessed what was up."

I almost wish I had caught whoever was following Callie. I'd beat the shit out of him, then use his confession to nail Fuchs. That fucking asshole.

"Mmm." Elliot's rubbing his chin. "Maybe. But that's a lot of effort."

"If he's willing to plant stories to strain my marriage in the hope of getting our shares, do you really think he'd stop at having Callie followed? Or listening in on her phone?"

Elliot pokes at Callie's phone, still sitting on his desk. "Do you think he's recording now?"

"No. I pulled out the battery this morning." Although he could've been tapping our first conversation, when I gave her the divorce papers. My hand curls into a fist as I imagine that sack of shit listening in on that painful, intimate moment.

Thank God I pulled the battery before Callie came up with the website idea. I don't want Fuchs to know about our scheme. I want this to hit him with the force of a Mack truck blindsiding him when our site launches. Just like he blindsided me.

"I'll get the phone to January right away," Elliot says.

"Thanks." I'm not one hundred percent convinced Fuchs spied on Callie through it, but I'll still be relieved when it's fixed. "Don't forget the LLC stuff. I'll announce it to all the guys at the Monday partners' meeting."

Elliot's mouth flattens. "Listen, Logan, I know everything seems great now, but just… be safe."

"What, like she'll kill me in my sleep?" I toss off the joke because I'm sick of Elliot doubting us.

He doesn't find it funny. "Seriously, if she leaves again…" *She's not getting a third chance from me*, his tone says. Hell, his attitude since we arrived says he's hardly giving her a second chance.

My breath catches. If she leaves again...

"I'll have to make sure that doesn't happen this time," I say with a lightness I don't feel. I get up and head for the door. I've kept Callie waiting long enough.

"Really? How?"

I turn, my hand on the doorknob. "She brought her cat with her."

That makes Elliot's jaw drop. "First, when did she get a cat? And second, how does that prove anything?"

I can't answer Elliot with logic—I only know deep in my gut that Callie's bringing along the cat means something. Yeah, she made a big fuss about not being able to get him out of the car, but that was bullshit. She *wanted* the cat to come.

And she wanted to come with me.

"Someday, baby bro, you'll understand women. And then you'll understand what I mean by the cat."

I shut the door while he's still spluttering about how I'm not making any damn sense and he knows plenty about women. I'm smiling as I cut him off.

## CHAPTER 11

He hasn't changed a thing about the house.

Walking into our shared home again has me trembling. I expected some things to be different and out of place and others to be painfully familiar.

After four months away, I didn't expect every last detail to be exactly the same.

I shouldn't be so surprised since Logan isn't the kind of guy to rearrange all the furniture, but when I say everything is the same, *everything* is the same.

The day before I left, there were some persimmons in a bowl on the kitchen table—the bowl is still filled with persimmons, fresh and ripe. Logan doesn't even like them.

The fridge is filled with the same foods I used to buy, although I doubt Logan has been cooking. My favorite throw is waiting on the couch, and my hair ties are still sitting on the side table. Meowthra wriggles out of my arms and hops onto the sofa, sniffing at the hair ties. He bites one, chewing for a moment, then drops it and curls up on the throw blanket.

Well, he's settling in nicely.

"I'll be right back," Logan says tightly, disappearing into his bedroom.

We technically have separate bedrooms, although in the early days of our marriage, I slept in his bed. As I saw him less and less though, I ended up in my room more often than not.

I go to my bedroom, already knowing what will be there. Nothing in my closet has been touched, although my things have all been dusted recently.

Logan never gave up hope I'd come back. He kept everything ready for the day I'd walk back in.

I look over the clothes hanging on the rods, the racks and racks of shoes, and the wall of purses. I might have gone a little crazy buying clothes when we first married, but I've always loved all kinds of design, including fashion design. Finally I could afford all the beautiful, stylish clothes I always longed for.

They beckon to me, calling to me to throw away the ratty sweater I'm wearing and put them on, to wrap myself in their luxurious elegance. I know that if I do, I'll immediately feel like a million dollars. There's nothing like a great outfit to make a woman feel awesome.

But I'm not ready for those clothes from my old life yet. Instead, I tuck myself deeper into my sweater and head out of the closet. There's something else I want to look for.

In the bathroom, I kneel on the marble floor and reach into the very back of my bathroom cabinet, past the hair spray and curling irons and blow-dryers, my hand closing on the small box hidden there. The edges cut into my palm, the box flexing under my grip.

It's the pregnancy test, the one I was going to take with Logan. The one I hid when I decided I was going to leave him. The design is pretty bland—white and blue stripes, the brand name big and bold, with smaller script touting the advanced science that went into the test. But I suppose the excitement of a pregnancy test comes from the test itself rather than the box.

The two tests inside rattle together; the box is still intact, never opened.

I don't need it, so I don't know why I had to go find it, but I did. It was an urge I couldn't ignore, to seek out that reminder of why I was so desperate to flee.

"Callie?"

My heart slams into my throat and I almost drop the box. I shove the test back into its hiding spot right before Logan walks in.

"Are you looking for something?"

I shake my head and shut the cabinet door. He hasn't seen the box, but I'm still shaky. "Just poking into stuff."

"I've got to go to work. I've been gone too long."

Of course. I know that he has to go in, even though we just came from there, and I don't want him glued to my side, but the old hurt still flares. I put a blank expression on my face. "Sure. I'm going to start on some graphics. We'll save some money on designs at least."

He doesn't even smile. His mouth is tight, his eyes narrow, like he's expecting me to bolt at any minute. Strangely, I don't have the urge to flee. I really do want to sit down and do some graphics work even if my stomach won't stop somersaulting.

This is my home, and yet it's not. This is my husband, and yet he's not. I feel like I've come through the looking glass. It'll take me a few days to get used to the right hand being the left.

"I'll see you when you get home," I say. I don't ask when that will be, and I'm proud of my willpower.

He stares a moment longer, then his hand snags my arm, tugging me into him. His mouth is on mine before I can even blink, his kiss like a brand. His lips move slow and sure against mine, like he's reminding me this is where I belong.

It feels right. So right that I kiss him back. The pull between us was always dazzling, dizzying, and it still is.

When he pulls back, there's a question in his eyes, clouding the navy blue of his irises. God, to see such uncertainty in a man like him…

"I'll be here," I say, my voice thick. "Don't worry."

He exhales, then releases my arm. "Call me if you need anything. There's a temporary phone in your office—I had it delivered."

Then he's gone.

I end up rubbing my arm for a long time after, trying not to think about how he didn't say how long he'd be gone. I didn't ask, so I shouldn't have expected an answer.

Finally I force myself to move and go do some work.

My office is also just as I left it. Logan made sure I'd have everything I need here—top-of-the-line graphics tablets, supersized high-def monitors, the fastest computers, and he even made sure the walls were painted a neutral color and the light was just so. If you're judging a color sample on a screen, those things are important, although most people don't know it.

Logan did though.

After a while, this office started to feel like a bad joke. I wasn't doing any design work, so why would I even need it?

But we didn't need the space—in this house, we have more than enough—and it felt wrong to tear apart what Logan built for me. But it also felt like he built it for an older version of Callie, one who ceased to exist once I became his wife.

Well, I'll need it now. I don't feel like the old Callie, but at least I'll be doing her work.

I plop down into the ergonomic chair, done up in custom

purple leather that had been Pantone's color of the year. I mentioned it to Logan as a color I really loved, so he had the chair made specially for me.

"Since everything else has to be colorless for your work, I can at least make the chair pretty," he said.

It really is a gorgeous color, deep, with a pop that makes my eyes widen. And it's the most comfortable chair I've ever had.

I take in the desk, which is mostly empty except for my graphics tablet and the phone Logan left. Of course the phone is the latest top-of-the-line model from Pixio, worth almost a thousand dollars. And it's supposed to be temporary.

"Hypatia," I call to the empty air.

"Welcome home." A robot voice responds from the speakers in the ceiling. "How may I help you, Calliope?"

Hypatia is Logan's electronic butler. She's the computer who runs the thermostat, the TV, the locks, the lighting, and everything else in our super-wired home. Logan let me name her and programmed her to always use my full name.

"Could you play some...?" I tap my chin, trying to decide what music fits my odd mood. "Some Beethoven."

Yes, some angsty Romantic symphonies are exactly what I need, all fire and bombast and rising tension. And then a heartbreaking drop.

Hypatia cues up the Third Symphony, and I pick up my stylus and graphics tablet. The weight feels strange in my hand after so long. But also right, like my hand wants to relearn these things.

I put the stylus to the screen and start sketching.

# CHAPTER 12

I try to breathe as I walk up to my front door, but my lungs won't let me.

*Let her be here. Let her be here.*

Callie's car has been delivered and is sitting in the garage, so she hasn't driven anywhere. But she could have walked down the hill, caught a bus, called a taxi, an Uber—there are any number of ways she could have left.

I won't know for certain until I'm inside and I see her.

It's past midnight. I wanted to be home earlier, but I couldn't get away. Elliot kept asking me about the LLC, I had a million and one emails to answer from anxious founders looking for my guidance, Dev wanted to meet about a prospectus he'd gotten, and…

And the hours slipped away until the day was over, but my workload wasn't. I never even found the time to tell everyone what happened with Callie. Mark and Finn weren't in the office—they had outside lives apparently—Paul was out at another meeting, Elliot already knew, and Dev didn't care.

So I'll have to tell them all tomorrow at the partners' meeting. Along with my—*our* plan to fight Fuchs. Again.

But first I need to make sure she hasn't left. Again.

Maybe that's why I didn't make an effort to contact the guys who were out of the office. I don't want to face them tomorrow if she's gone and I told them she was here.

No, that's not right. They're my brothers; they'd always be on my side. I wouldn't want to face *myself*, knowing that Fuchs's lies were too strong for her to overcome. Knowing that seeing our life together again wasn't enough to convince her to stay.

The door lock clicks as I walk up, the electronics in it recognizing the fob on my keys.

"Welcome home," Hypatia says as I walk in, the lights in the foyer automatically coming up.

"Is—" I stop myself before I ask my computer if my wife is home.

"Yes?" Hypatia says, eternally patient.

"Nothing."

I toss my jacket, briefcase, and keys on the end table in the entry. I don't see any sign of Callie yet. Except…

My nose twitches. Is that roast chicken?

It's been so long since I've smelled anything cooking in my kitchen I can't tell if I'm hallucinating. I don't cook, so I haven't even walked into the kitchen since Callie left. I made sure the housekeeper kept the kitchen stocked with exactly what Callie had there when she left. But I never bothered to check that it was done.

The lights come up in the kitchen and living room as I walk in, flooding the space with illumination.

"Logan?" Callie's head pops up from the sofa, long strands of hair tangled around her shoulders and arms. She pushes it out of her face as she blinks sleepily. "You're home."

Jesus. She waited up for me. She's never done that before. Guilt twists hard through me. "You should have gone to bed. You're exhausted."

"Yeah," she says idly. "I made some chicken and rice."

"Did you eat?"

"I was going to." She yawns again, covering it with her long fingers. Which are stained with ink.

Fucking A. She waited for me to eat and then she fell asleep on the couch, and judging by her fingers, she was probably working all day too. "You have to eat. And sleep. You can't do this to yourself."

Her hand drops, and she stares steadily at me. "But you can do it to yourself?"

"That's not the point." Christ, not this again. I wasted two days of work finding her. I've got to fit those two days back into my schedule now since the work sure as shit didn't stop while I was gone.

I hold on to my temper though because she's not ready to accept my work schedule yet. And I did mean to come home earlier than this. It just didn't happen.

"Then what is?" she asks. She spreads her arms wide, as if she'd gather up everything in the house if she could. "What is the point of all this?"

"The point is to provide for you." My voice is cold and jagged as an icicle. Why the hell doesn't she appreciate what I've done for her? That office, her bedroom, her yoga studio, this entire house—I liked our house, sure, but I built it for her.

"It's Sunday. And—" She shakes her head as she looks at the clock on the wall. "Actually, it's Monday now. You'll be back in the office in less than eight hours."

"Yes. But I'm here now."

"Good." She rises briskly from the couch. "Then we can eat."

While she prepares plates for us, I open a bottle of wine to breathe.

"Where's that from?" Callie points to the label. "It looks familiar."

"It should. That's your design, and this is from your winery."

She pauses halfway to the table, a plate in each hand. "My winery."

"Yep." I fill two long-stemmed glasses. "Remember that?"

She sets the plates down a little too hard. "How could I forget?" She snags a glass from me and takes a long drink. "Out of nowhere, you bought me a winery."

I sit down, holding her gaze the entire time. "Why do you act like everything I do for you is now an insult? You weren't complaining when I built this house. Or when you had all day to do whatever you wanted. Or even when I gave you the winery—not a word."

She sits down during that speech, then stabs a piece of chicken. "No, I left. Which I thought sent a pretty clear message." She stabs another piece but doesn't bring the fork to her mouth. "That was always your problem—you thought you could buy things to keep me happy."

I take a long drink from my own wineglass, the better to cool my temper. My mother would have been really fucking happy had someone—like my father—bought her things. Like groceries. Or paid the rent.

"Should I send all this back?" I ask coolly. "Would that finally make you happy, to be living like you were before?"

She flinches, because she was on the razor's edge of poverty in the City before, and she knows it. As more money flows into this place, the more it takes to keep a person afloat here. And the salary of a graphic designer isn't much.

I'm not going to apologize for giving the people I love nice things. Beautiful things. Oh, and keeping a roof over their head and food in their stomach.

"No, I wouldn't." She takes a bite, defiance in her expression. "But I also don't want to live like *we* were before."

I force myself to soften, because I don't want her to leave again. Fighting with her over our first dinner together in months isn't going to help me. "I really did mean to come home before this."

"But you didn't." She stabs another bite of chicken. And then she drops her fork. "Work was crazy, huh?"

Resignation blurs her voice. But the resentment has been smoothed out.

"It's always crazy," I say. I can't change that or the nature of what I do. The tech world is set up to go twenty-four seven, and I have to go that much too if I want to keep up. I gesture to the food. "This is really good."

Callie actually brightens. "Thanks. I found the recipe a while ago, and there was a whole chicken in the fridge—" She bites her lip. "You don't cook, but there was a ton of food in there."

I shrug. "Maybe one day I might want to try it."

Or maybe I was waiting this whole time for her to come home and take possession of what was hers. Including all the food in the house.

I'm trying to keep my expression neutral, but something must give me away, because she pinches up her mouth like she's going to cry.

Fuck. Her crying during our first dinner together in a while is worse than us arguing.

But she wrestles her mouth flat. Our gazes meet, and something... that hot, crazy *something* flares between us.

Her gaze runs over me, going from cool to hot. Energy surges through me, all the dirt from the day washed away as I soak in her expression.

I set down my fork. "I'm not hungry anymore."

She swallows hard. Oh, she's definitely hungry—for what

we're both thinking of. There isn't a hint of hesitation or regret in her eyes—I might have insisted she share my bed, but she definitely wants to be there.

"I'm done," she says, her voice breathless.

"Good." There's a growl in my voice I didn't mean to put there, my desire slipping its leash. "Let's go to bed."

Her eyes darken and her cheeks flush. "Your bed?"

She's not asking because she's uncertain about joining me —the pulse in her throat is eager, not frightened, and the pink of her cheeks is enticing, not anxious.

I walk over to her chair, slowly. Stalking her. "Yes."

She shifts, her limbs spreading as if in welcome. "That's what I thought."

I pull her into my arms, her mouth finding mine. She smells of roses and warm sleep, and home. I tried to keep the house exactly as she left it, but this is what was missing, what I could never replicate—her scent.

I kiss her until we're both panting, then I pull her into my arms. For the first time in a long time, she's going to sleep in my bed.

Right where she belongs.

## CHAPTER 13

I wanted to be so angry when Logan came home.

Stupid me, not putting conditions on when he had to be home, how much he could work. In my defense, I've never negotiated anything, and I was going up against a master.

I *was* angry as I watched the dinner I made go cold, as I lay down on the couch to wait for him.

But when he came home and woke me up, I forgot to be angry. And when he said he meant to be home earlier... I melted.

He's never done that before. Maybe... maybe he really was trying this time.

Right now he's kissing me like it's our very first time, his arms tight around me as he carries me to his bed. There's no *try* here, just *want* and *need* and *finally.*

We have on too many clothes. I'm desperate to feel his skin, shaking with my need. I want him on me and over me and in me, now.

"Hurry," I murmur. Then I bite his lower lip to get my message across.

He makes a noise somewhere between a gasp and growl. "You want me." His voice is gritty. "You always wanted me."

Oh, Logan. He has to be right, even when I'm begging him to fuck me. But I'm not going to roll over so easily. I might be sleeping with him—or about to—but he can get home early tomorrow instead of *trying*.

"I ran," I remind him. "And hid from you."

"You didn't run very far." He bites my lip, just hard enough to remind me that his teeth are sharp. "You didn't hide very well." He starts to unbutton his shirt, his gaze hard, daring. "You wanted me to chase you, find you."

"No," I say without thinking, mostly because I don't want him to win this fight.

But… maybe. Maybe I did want him to chase me. Maybe I wanted his attention again and figured that was the best way to get it.

I certainly have his attention now, and I want to bask in it like Meowthra in a sunbeam.

Logan lets his shirt drop to the floor, then reaches for the button on his pants. I grab his hands before he finds it.

I want to do this myself. I need to touch him.

The skin of his belly against my knuckle is warm, rough with hair. The muscles there are hard and stark, contracting and releasing with his breaths. I have to simply stop and stare.

I catch sight of the small smile on Logan's face and realize I've been staring openmouthed long enough for him to notice.

"Did you forget something?" he rasps.

With a flick of my thumb, his button releases. We inhale in unison, and then Logan is kicking away his pants, sliding his boxers down his legs. And then he comes to me in all his naked beauty.

We step together toward the bed, our legs moving in a well-remembered dance. I let him get one step ahead so I can drink him in. I've missed the sight of him almost as much as I've missed his kisses.

His body is simply glorious. When the Greeks were making all their statues of the ideal male form, Logan's body was what they were trying to capture. The perfect balance of muscle and function and beauty.

He's not embarrassed to have me stare at him like this, and why should he be? My mother always said he was too good-looking, as if that were a crime, but I thought his looks were a gift. Just for me, back when I knew he loved me.

I take another step back, suddenly confused. What do I mean, *when I knew he loved me?*

Logan isn't confused though. He catches me before I fall back on the bed, taking all my weight in his arms. His mouth finds my chin, my jaw, my ear, and he makes little murmurs all the way, as if each kiss is a new delight he's found.

My whole body is clamoring for him, especially my pussy. I can't deny myself, not after months without him. Not that I need to, not with our agreement.

I run my hands down his chest, over his arms, remembering all the details of him. The smattering of springy hair on his pecs, his nipples, which come to attention at my touch, and the scar under his rib from a car wreck.

His hands on me are urgent but controlled, a man carrying out a long-planned siege. I'm ready to fall after only a few minutes though.

He pulls off my sweater without warning, leaving me in only a tank top and leggings. Suddenly I'm freezing, my body curling in on itself as my teeth chatter. The room isn't cold though, so I can't understand why I'm shivering.

Logan tosses back the blankets on the bed, guides me down to it, then covers my body with his. The chills slow, then stop.

"Are you okay?" he asks, his voice a rough scrape.

I nod because this roller coaster I'm on has made my voice too shaky to use. And I don't want to talk. I want to feel.

Logan's hand slips under my tank, his palm rough and warm and so surprising I gasp. The song "Like a Virgin" takes on a whole new meaning right now.

I'm squirming by the time he reaches my breasts because his path upward is so damn methodical and slow. My heart is loud in my ears, and I can't seem to draw a full breath, I'm so worked up.

When he finds my nipple, I almost scream.

I hardly ever wear a bra—I've never been well endowed enough to need one. Right now it seems like the luckiest thing ever that Logan can simply reach under my shirt and find my breasts, my aching nipples, drawing them to firm, tight points.

I grab his shoulder and dig my nails in, ready for him to fill me. All he has to do is caress my nipples and my pussy is soaked and throbbing, hollow without him.

But Logan won't be hurried. He keeps tormenting me by touching my breasts, teasing one nipple, then the other, his every movement precision engineered to drive me to the edge.

I put my hand at his shoulder and push. He resists but only for half a heartbeat. When he raises his head, his expression is wild, confused.

I grab the hem of my tank and pull it over my head, tossing it aside. I do the same with my boots and leggings until I'm as naked as he is.

Although less blasé about it. As I lie back on the bed, Logan remains on his knees, watching me. Since his body isn't covering mine, I have to cover it with my own hands.

I've always been what you'd call gangly. Always the tallest, thinnest kid in school. I used to wonder if I might be part stick insect.

Then I hit puberty, and suddenly my body was what society called the sexiest of all. I couldn't understand it since I was still skinny and tall as ever, except now with some hints of breasts, and of course, I was only a teenager.

Men didn't seem to care though. They hit on me anyway. They never saw that I was still only a kid, that I was horribly embarrassed and shy and scared. And I hated them for not seeing that. I hated them for their complete lack of control around me.

It got better as I got older and more confident. When I met Logan, I met the one man who looked at me with equal parts lust and control.

I could be free and safe with him—when I could be with him.

He's here with me now though, and I'm going to seize this moment and squeeze all the pleasure out of it. I don't know what we'll do tomorrow, but for now this is enough.

So I move my hands, let Logan look his fill at me.

He doesn't say anything, but he doesn't need to. I can see it in his eyes, how much he missed this. Missed me.

Of course we never had problems in the bedroom. No, everything always came together perfectly there.

Logan takes my knees and spreads my thighs wide. I grab for the sheets, bracing myself for what's coming. Already I'm shivering with anticipation, my calves quivering with it.

When he leans over and licks my pussy, I make the most insane noise, deep in my throat. It's like months and months of sexual frustration is unraveling and rattling my voice box.

Logan doesn't slow down, his clever tongue lapping at my most sensitive parts, his lips teasing my clit. My head thrashes on the pillow, my fists wrapped tight in the sheets, yet he won't let me catch my breath, won't let the pleasure ease for even a moment.

I'm all wild, uncontained sensation by the time I come, pushed to the edge and beyond by this man who knows me too well.

When I open my eyes, he's braced above me, his expression stark, his gaze burning.

"Are you still on the pill?"

I nod, and then he's pushing forward, his cock filling me. It's been so long I'm tight as a glove around him. He groans, stops, and shakes his head as if to clear it. Then he's moving again, filling me so perfectly I want to die like this, pleasure-soaked and consumed by this man.

He's as relentless as he was when he was licking my pussy, driving, driving, driving until we're both gasping and sweating, pushing hard toward our climax. I want to bite him, to claw him, to be as wild as the sensations churning in me.

Logan is my mate. We're mating. Primitive words, but they feel so right.

When I come the second time, my pussy clenching around his cock as my eyes roll back, it's even more powerful than the first, because this time we're joined. He's with me, and it makes it that much more potent.

I feel heat spill inside me, spreading throughout my core as he comes too. I've always loved that part of married sex, even though it's not proper to enjoy it. I'm too damn pleased to care about proper though.

We're both breathing too hard, sweat coating our skin, and we… we *smile* at each other. I don't even know who smiled first, just that we both did in the end.

And somehow that moment feels more intimate than the carnal, sensual ones before.

## CHAPTER 14

Waking up in Logan's bed is both surprising and familiar.

Weak light is coming through the floor-to-ceiling windows covering one entire wall of his bedroom. It looks like the fog is going to stick around today.

I stretch, not bothering to watch out for Logan. I already know that he's gone. The sheets are colder than when he was here, the air staler. Everything will be chilled and still until he comes home tonight, the way it was yesterday.

Once my kinks are out, I sigh and let my shoulders slump. I ran through several branding ideas yesterday, including some fonts teasing through my brain, but another day of simply staring at my sketches doesn't really sound appealing. I *do* want to work, but I also want to get out, see the City. See my friends.

That thought makes my skin break out in goose bumps. I'll have to tell them I'm back with Logan. Temporarily. I think.

I bury my face in my hands, but I can't find any relief there. Last night was awful and amazing all at once. Awful because I made dinner and waited for Logan like an idiot. And of course he didn't come home until late.

But amazing once he had me in bed, under him, as we moved together. And the orgasms… My body is still tingling this morning.

So we're already back to Logan being gone all the time and the two of us only having quality time in bed.

I drop my hands, force some steel into my spine. It's only been one day—things could still change. I'm just not sure how yet.

I pull on my old sweater over my T-shirt and yoga pants, then head into the kitchen.

Someone's put away the food I left out last night, which I should have thought of myself.

A mug of tea is already waiting for me, the lovely blend I couldn't get in Platina. It's only sold here in the City, and I've missed it desperately. There's a plate of croissants waiting too, with several chocolate-dipped strawberries nestled against them. This is a breakfast fit for a princess.

I take the mug between my hands and breathe deeply, feeling as if I'm waking to a fairy tale. Like Cinderella the morning after a nightmare about her stepmother and cleaning out the hearth, realizing the Prince Charming she'd dreamed of before is real and this is her life now.

Except… the prince is gone for the day and the castle is big and empty and with all these servants, there's not much to do. Not if all you know how to do is sweeping and cleaning and general drudgery.

I already know what Logan is doing. It's eight a.m. on a Monday, which means the partners' meeting is in two hours. All the Bastards will assemble and discuss their week—what their pet companies are doing, how much money they made last week, which deals and how much money they expect to make this week. I've never attended one of their meetings, but I've imagined them often.

Logan would never miss one, no more than he'd miss

Christmas or Thanksgiving. Actually, he'd be more likely to miss a holiday than a partners' meeting.

He's going to bring up everything that happened with *TidBytes* and my proposal to fight Fuchs with his own weapons. They'll tear apart his ideas, probably talk him out of starting our own news site.

I sit straight up. No, they'll tear apart *my* ideas. I had to fight to get Logan to go along with this—will he fight for me to continue it?

That was part of our deal, but those are his brothers. They might be able to talk him into anything. If he abandons the idea...

I could leave again, but I don't want to. I want my website, and I want my husband.

I've never attended one of their meetings, never wanted to, but I want to fight for my plan. Fight for my place in Logan's life, when it comes down to it. I have a right to be at that meeting if they're discussing my ideas.

"Mrs. Martell?"

I jump and spin on the stool to find the housekeeper standing behind me.

"Mary!" I smile widely with relief. "You're still here."

She nods, her answering smile uncertain. "I'm so glad you're back. Your things arrived today." She discreetly clears her throat, her discomfort at my messy marriage situation almost getting the better of her. "Would you like to unpack them today? I'll help."

It's what Cinderella would have done, taken the day to reclaim her castle and fill it with her things. It's what I should do instead of poking my nose into the parts of Logan's life where I don't belong.

"Actually, I have a meeting I have to get to," I say. "You can leave them for now."

"Of course. Is there anything else you need?"

"Yes." My mind is spinning with ideas, things I want to get done right now. "Could you arrange for a caterer for a late-afternoon meeting here? I'm going to have some people over to discuss a venture I'm starting."

"You are?" Her eyes widen as she realizes how skeptical she made that sound.

I can't blame her. Logan is the venture capitalist, not me. I don't have meetings here, because what could I possibly be doing that would require meetings?

"Yep." I smile to let her know I'm not offended. "It's unusual, but there are going to be a lot of changes around here."

"Well…" She pulls herself a little taller. "I'm glad. Things were not so good when you were gone."

They were not so good when I was last here. Logan coming home so late and disappearing this morning doesn't give me hope that they'll change this time either.

"Thank you for taking care of the house," I say. "It looks wonderful."

"He wanted me to keep it exactly like you left it."

I know that, having seen it last night, but hearing her say it makes my chest tighten. "Thank you," I say with quiet strain.

"Should I make you something for breakfast?"

I blink, grateful that she's changed the subject. Things were getting too painful there. "Maybe." I glance at the clock, then start. "Oh no, I have to get going."

I wave to her as I race to my bedroom, then tear into my closet. It's going to take some time to pick out what I want to wear, then do my makeup.

If I'm going into a business meeting as a partner, I need to look the part.

# CHAPTER 15

"Look who the cat dragged in."

I glance up from my computer screen—I've been staring at the damn thing for almost three hours—to see Mark standing in my office. Mark's smile is wide, but then that asshole's been nonstop grinning since he and January got together.

I wonder if this is how the rest of them felt when I married Callie. Surly and jealous and wishing I didn't have to rub it in.

"Fuck off," I say in greeting. "I didn't see you here yesterday."

"That bad?" Mark's voice drops to a gentler, more understanding register. He knows I found Callie and about the legal papers I took with me.

It's definitely not bad, but... Yes, Callie's home with me again, which was my goal—seriously, fuck those divorce papers—but she's not *happy*. Her reaction when I came home last night made that clear. But what happened after...

"She's home."

Mark picks up on my lack of triumph. "What happened?"

"Fuchs fucking with us again is what happened. Elliot told you about *TidBytes*?"

Mark's nod is grim. "Not in detail, but yeah. Using a gossip blog against us is some pretty weak shit."

"Wait until I tell you my plan to stop him," I say dryly. "The partners' meeting is going to be a blast."

"If it gives Fuchs a black eye, I'm all for it."

Convincing Mark on the gossip site won't be hard—Fuchs went hard after January a while back, and Mark's still pissed he couldn't bury Fuchs. Like literally.

I can totally sympathize. If we get our wish, we can take turns with the shovel.

My computer dings—it's time to assemble in the conference room. And then it shifts to howling, then an alarm, and finishes off with a siren. Anjie used to have to corral most of us into meetings, like a mom waking up teenagers for school. Then she came up with the alarm, and now nobody's late.

"Finn disabled his," Mark says, looking like he's eaten the audio equivalent of some rotten socks.

"It *is* fucking embarrassing. We're Bastard Capital."

"Alarms? We don't need no stinking alarms!"

I exchange a glance with Mark. "Are you going to disable yours?"

"Hell, no. I'm not going to piss off Anjie."

"Me either." I clap Mark on the shoulder. "Speaking of which, we'd better go."

As we walk to the conference room, Anjie pops her head out of the staff kitchen. "Logan? You're back!"

She hugs me, hard, and I let her. Anjie is our office manager, den mom, and the one person who keeps us all on track. Without her, we'd have never made it out of that garage and into this building on Sand Hill Road.

Anjie takes my shoulders and studies me. She's into retro

styles, and today she looks like she should be at the starting line of an illegal drag race.

"I'm glad she came back," Anjie says, reading what happened in my face.

"Yeah." I try to be more upbeat with Anjie than with Mark. "We're trying again." *Because I forced her to.*

This is a hell of time for my conscience to reappear. I tell it to take a flying leap.

Mark says nothing, his face blank.

"I'm so happy for you." Anjie squeezes my shoulders. "Tell her to come visit me when she gets a chance."

"Sure," I say. But Callie isn't likely to come back to the office anytime soon. She never liked coming in after we were married.

Anjie claps her hands, her expression going teacherly. "Okay, everyone in the conference room."

Within minutes, Anjie's got everyone corralled in their usual seats, coffee and tea and fruit and pastries sitting out. Seriously, the woman is magical. Maybe even a goddess.

Elliot, who's got a bug up his ass from yesterday, sits next to me, his mood like a rain cloud over his head.

Paul shoots his cuffs as he looks between the two of us. "Everything okay?"

"I'll let Logan explain."

I roll my eyes. Elliot can do pissy like no one else. "Thanks, baby bro."

The table breaks out in laughter as Elliot shakes his head in exasperation.

"Sooo." Finn adds a million *o*'s to that. "What did happen?"

"There was a misunderstanding. But Callie's home now."

Elliot snorts while the rest of them look completely unconvinced. They're all still pissed that Callie left me without a word. What they don't understand is that that didn't make her my enemy.

And they never really got to know her, which didn't help. She was uncomfortable with them, and they were uncomfortable with her, so we never really all spent time together. Keeping your home life separate from work is what a lot of dudes do. It never struck me as something to fix.

Maybe this time around I should. I was the first one of us to have a really serious relationship, the first to get married. In my defense, I had no idea what would happen.

The Bastards still aren't saying anything, although Anjie is glaring daggers at them. She's definitely rooting for forgiving Callie.

I grab Elliot's shoulder and squeeze, although I address all of them. "Be happy for me." I make that a command. And a plea. I need these guys on Callie's side, because if they're not on her side, they're not on mine. "Shit happened that neither of us could control. It's not her fault."

"Whose fault is it?" Paul breaks the too-long silence with that question.

"Fuchs," I say. *And mine.*

Seriously, my conscience needs to shut it.

"Again?" Finn asks. "What's that motherfucker's problem?"

Dev, at the head of the table, steeples his fingers. He's the thinker, the philosopher. Mark's our dealmaker, Finn's our genius, Paul's our money guy, and Elliot's our lawyer.

I'm the details guy. I catch shit that other people miss. Unless it involves my wife, I guess. I missed all that shit, including a goddamn pregnancy scare.

I'm not going to miss anything this time. I can do eighty-hour weeks here and still have time for her. She's wrong, and I just need to work harder to prove it to her. And maybe make it home earlier tonight.

Dev taps his fingers together. "What happened?"

"Well, you all know and love *TidBytes*," I say.

Mark pulls a face like he's about to puke.

"Fuchs owns it. All those pictures and stories they run on us? Yeah, that's all Fuchs. Trying to fuck with us. With Callie and me."

"Aw, man," Finn says. "I thought they actually liked us, that that's why we're in there all the time."

I can't tell if he's joking or not. "Anyway, Callie saw all those pictures of me at parties, the ones where other women so conveniently happened to be in the frame, and it upset her."

There's another long beat of silence, again broken by Paul. "Because of that, she left you without a word, only communicated through Julian, and was missing for months?"

"There were some other things," I say blandly, chilled. "But we're working through them."

The work stuff is just Callie projecting other issues onto my schedule—these guys would never understand cutting back on work hours—and Callie would never forgive me if I told them about the pregnancy scare. Or her hopes for what a baby would mean to us.

None of these guys are even close to getting married except for maybe Mark. It'd be like speaking pig latin to them.

Finally Mark smiles and leans back in his chair. "I'm glad you guys are trying again."

The tension doesn't quite dissolve, but it does crack.

"If you're happy," Finn says, "then I guess it's good."

"Good luck," Paul says.

Anjie grins like I told her she won the lottery, and Elliot sends a look that says, *I'm not happy, but I'm also not saying anything.*

Dev still has his hands together, his expression distant.

Like he's meditating or something. "I want to go back to Fuchs."

"Yeah, I haven't finished telling you everything. I gave Callie the divorce papers"—Anjie makes a noise like a wounded kitten—"and the next morning *TidBytes* has the divorce on the front page and Minerva Dyne is on her doorstep, offering to buy Callie's shares in Bastard Capital once the divorce is final."

"Son of a bitch," Finn shouts.

"Don't worry, the divorce is off the table."

"Not permanently," Elliot mutters under his breath.

I ignore him. "Fuchs clearly has an agenda here, and he's using his stupid gossip site as a weapon. Using it to fuck with my marriage. And to slither his way into our firm."

Every expression becomes flinty, because fuck that. This is our Alamo, and we're fighting to the last man. Fuck, I'll burn the place down before I let Fuchs own a piece of it.

"We need to put this fucker down like a rabid dog." Mark stabs the table for emphasis.

"Seriously. I know some places in the desert," Finn says. "Nobody will ever find him."

Paul laughs while Elliot pretends not to hear. I guess he needs plausible deniability or something.

Dev unfolds his hands. "So he's declared war on us?" Dev's clearly skeptical of the theory, probably because he'd never do anything so messy as seek out revenge.

Paul snorts. "Have you met the guy? He's missing some empathy chips. And some humanity chips. He's read too much crappy fantasy. He thinks he's some kind of elvish warrior on a quest and we're trolls to be squashed."

"What is it with these guys and elves?" Finn asks. He's always been for the trolls, the dirtbags, the blue-collar guys.

"What's not to love?" Mark asks. "Pointy ears, long blond hair, dying race."

We all laugh. We're definitely not on the side of the elves or anyone else in this town who thinks they're supermen, disrupting the world for good.

We're Bastards. It's right there in the name.

And Fuchs is about to find out just how big a bastard I can be.

## CHAPTER 16

This time when I walk through the offices of Bastard Capital, I don't bother to look at any of the associates, not even from the corner of my eye.

Someone who belonged here wouldn't, and so I won't. I'm twenty minutes late for the partners' meeting, but getting myself into this state—hair blow-dried perfectly straight and silky smooth, my makeup noticeably tasteful, and my outfit chic and sleek—took longer than I expected.

I have on a red leather skirt with a heavy buckle and some zippers, just enough to say "Don't mess with me" instead of "I really like punk rock." Since the skirt is so much, I paired it with a plain black shirt with a ballerina neckline. My watch is delicate and rose gold, while my earrings dangle all the way to my shoulders, studded with tiny diamonds. I finished the look with high-heeled, open-toed black suede booties, and my manicured toes peep out at me with every step.

No expense was spared with my clothes, and I look it. But as I push open the conference room doors, I wish I had my old sweater instead so I could curl up in it.

The doors swing open wide. Every face turns to me.

None of them are happy to see me.

I set my jaw even as my pulse kicks up. It's totally fine, because I wasn't expecting them to be happy. Except for Anjie—she's already getting up, coming over to hug me.

I definitely missed her. She was the one person in this office I could actually talk to, besides Logan.

"We're so glad you're back," she says. "And we want you to stay." She whispers that only for my ears.

She says *we*, but the Bastards don't want to be included in her welcome. I can already tell from their expressions.

"Callie," Mark says, all smooth suaveness. I never trusted Mark—he was always too slick, always the dealmaker. "What a surprise."

Logan rises from his chair, comes over to me. "Callie." His gaze is dark as it roams over me, and I'm suddenly very glad I took the time to get ready. "You don't have to worry about this. I'll handle it."

His hand comes to my elbow, pulling us into a circle of just us two, shutting out the rest of the Bastards. With the right kind of look—slow, sultry—I could lure him out of here and have him follow me home.

But this place is his real home. And these are his brothers. He'll only leave me to come back. I have to find a way to fit that into our marriage.

Oh, and we also have a ton of work to do, together.

"You're wrong," I say. "Fuchs targeted me too. And I'm involved in this blog, so I should be in this meeting."

There's a long beat of silence. And then, "*Blog?*"

When I look past Logan, they're all staring with shock. And not the good kind.

Finn was the one who yelled out *blog,* and he's not finished. "Blogs are dead. Only *mommies* blog anymore."

Meaning women. And not the hip kind he'd concern himself with. Blogs are only a place for mothers to post charming stories about potty training.

Finn's never been part of a blog community, never poured out his stories in the hopes of connecting with someone across the internet. That's *girl stuff.*

I'm tempted to give him my traffic numbers from *The Silicon Wife*, just to see the look on his face. He'd say *blog* very differently then.

I give Logan a gentle push so that he's not standing between me and the rest of them. "If blogs are so dead, why are you all freaking out about one right now?"

"*TidBytes* is more than a blog," Dev says.

"Right." I set a hand on my hip, straighten my shoulders. I'm wearing a power outfit, and I need the stance to go with it. "*TidBytes* taps into one of the deepest human impulses— sharing stories about your neighbor. Gossip. That impulse is primitive, centered around communities, so you tech boys reject it. But you need it."

Finn is spluttering, Elliot looks like I accused him of murder, but Logan is laughing. Dev and Paul join in after a moment.

I don't think I've ever seen them laughing together before. At least not at something I said. Usually we search for conversation for a while, and then they pull Logan away while I find something else to do. Or I pull Logan away first.

"She's right," Anjie says. "Remember what we used against Fuchs last time? Not just January's program, but gossip too."

A look passes between her and Dev, quick and bright as a spark.

Before I can analyze that look, Logan is nudging me. "Tell them the rest of it."

My confidence wants to leak right out of the soles of my booties as I stare back at the Bastards. They invest in companies that will be worth billions someday, things like self-driving cars and computers that can see into the future and things I can't even dream of.

Not something as small as what I'm imagining.

But *TidBytes* is a small thing, and Arne Fuchs tried to use it to ruin my marriage. Which isn't small to me at all.

"We're going to build a competitor to *TidBytes*." I say that strong and firm. "Better stories, more addictive content, more viral memes. We're going to build the one site that Silicon Valley can't do without, the kind that you laugh over with your coworkers, whisper about with your closest friends. The site you check first thing in the morning and last thing before bed."

It sounds so much bigger when I put it like that.

"But… we don't do that," Elliot says.

I can't tell if Elliot is talking about building a website or gossiping. Either would fit him.

"We're going to do it together. Which is why I need to be in this meeting."

Logan puts a hand to the small of my back, a simple gesture that any husband might do. But in front of these guys, it means something more: *We're in this together, she and I.*

I lean into his hand, taking strength from him and letting him know that I appreciate the gesture.

Something shifts at the table. Their wall against me isn't gone, but they've opened the door. And it's up to me to walk through.

First I need to find a seat at the table. I give Elliot a pointed look. He gets up and moves over, leaving the seat next to Logan's empty.

I take it, trying not to let my hands shake as I pull out my laptop. I'm not half as confident as I'm pretending to be.

Logan settles in next to me, solid and big. And his aftershave…

Nope. I'm not going to let how yummy he smells distract me.

"All right." Dev is addressing me. "What's the plan here?"

They're all looking at me, not Logan. Somehow I've been put in charge. Which is what I wanted. I think.

"We, um, hire people. Journalists."

There's no response. That answer wasn't enough. I lick my lips, try to remember my practiced spiel. I have so much I want to say, and I can't remember any of it.

"And then we find a name…"

I lick my lips again. Nobody is saying anything or offering the slightest bit of encouragement. I've walked through the door, but they're still not welcoming me. I wonder if they give this treatment to whoever comes begging them for money. But I don't need their money—I need their support. Both for this project and my marriage.

Logan clears his throat. "We'll need coders—not anybody too heavy hitting, it's only a website—and we'll need writers, designers, and we'll need the ears of everyone we know in the Valley. Seriously, it won't be half as hard as it looks."

I blink at my laptop screen, resisting the urge to gape at Logan. Here I was, worried he'd let them talk him out of this, but he's defending the idea even better than I am.

Paul drums his fingers against the table. "No, I think you're right. It might just work. *TidBytes* is almost a hate read at this point. If we have a better alternative, it's going to get under Fuchs's skin. I *love* the idea of that."

Mark nods, his expression wolfish.

"I still like the lawsuit," Elliot says. He's still grumpy. Or rather, he's still grumpier than usual. I've always wondered how he and Logan can share DNA since they certainly don't share personality traits.

"That's because you have no imagination," Logan says with rough affection. They might not share any traits, but they definitely love each other.

I've never known what it's like to have a sibling, but I do envy Logan and Elliot their bond.

Mark leans back in his chair. "A lawsuit would be bad PR. Even though *TidBytes* is trash, you'll get people screaming about the free press or whatever. Starting a competitor makes us look like we care about the freedom of information, the public's right to know."

"We don't?" I ask. I'm not used to that amount of cynicism in my work.

"Of course we do." Logan rolls his eyes. "Mark's just doing his asshole impression."

"It's not an impression," Finn says. "He really is an asshole."

Mark happily flips off Finn, who flips him off back.

I've never seen them act like this before. Whenever I would visit the office, they'd be stiff, unwelcoming. And I definitely wouldn't stay long, just long enough to drag Logan out.

They came to the house for parties and such, but again, they'd pull Logan aside, cutting me out of their charmed circle.

Maybe we were both fighting for Logan's attention back then.

"One thing that we don't need to do is hire a graphic designer," I say as I flip my laptop around. I might not know how to run a meeting or set up a website, but I do have some skills. "I've already started to play with logos and layouts. I want it to feel fun, playful, maybe a little naughty. Like these are all the Silicon Valley stories you're not supposed to know, but we're letting you in on the secret."

"I like that one." Finn points to a design with the lower half of a man's face—he's got a beard—and leaning close with painted nails is the lower half of a woman's face, her red lips whispering to him. Finn tugs on his own beard. "It's sexy."

I have to laugh, because Finn's humor is infectious. "Yeah, that was kind of the point."

We share a smile. Why couldn't Finn have been so welcoming before?

"That's one thing we can check off," Dev says dryly. "What about all the rest?"

"Callie will work from home," Logan says. "We can set up the main offices in the space in SoMa."

"Not the RWC facility?" Paul asks.

"Not necessary. We won't need that much security."

I raise my hand, feeling like a school kid interrupting the teachers. "Excuse me, but what facilities and spaces are you talking about?"

Finn stabs Logan with a look. "You never told her about our buildings?"

"Buildings? You guys own buildings, like multiple? Beyond this one?"

Logan takes a deep inhale. "No, I didn't tell her because why would she want to know?"

I go very still. He's right—before I wouldn't have cared much how many buildings Bastard Capital owned. I'm a graphic designer, and that's all VC stuff. Logan's domain.

But I'm more than a graphic designer now—I'm a *founder*, and I want to know more about everything they do.

"Tell me about the buildings," I say to Logan. "I want to know where our team will be working."

"There's the secure facility in RWC where we had January's team, but that won't work for a media company." Logan taps his pen against the table, his fingers long and graceful. "We need something more welcoming. The space on Second Street should work."

He's named a place right in the very heart of SoMa, where there's a cluster of tech companies. Real estate there isn't cheap, even by San Francisco standards.

"If I'm at home," I say slowly, realization hitting me, "and the company is in SoMa, where will you be?"

We're supposed to be a team on this, right? Me and Logan, doing this together.

"Here." He makes it sound like there was never any question of where he'd work, and I suppose there never was. After all, I can't expect him to set up a desk right next to mine.

"Good," I say crisply. "We'll need a presence in Silicon Valley proper as well, maybe a satellite office there."

"I can look into that," Anjie offers.

"We can't forget the actual employees," Logan says. "Maybe get on Twitter, see if we can bring up any freelance tech writers looking for something more permanent. There's got to be a ton of guys out there hustling."

"Don't forget the ladies," I say. They all turn to me. "I know a ton of women who'd be great writers. Women with awesome educations who know the Valley inside and out. Women looking for maybe more to do."

I'm thinking specifically of my commenters on *The Silicon Wife*, although I can't actually say that. But also my friends from my old life, the designers and artists who have just as much to contribute to tech as brogrammers do.

"Like who?" Paul isn't aggressive when he asks—more like he can't imagine who I might be describing.

I take a deep breath. "Well, to start with… like the wives of everyone you know."

## CHAPTER 17

When I arrive home, I'm feeling pretty smug. It's only eight o'clock—there's no way Callie will be upset with me for getting home *this* early. And I left a shitload of work still to be done, which is making the back of my brain itch. I try to ignore it and focus on how happy Callie will be to see me.

When I open the front door, I hear a noise that makes me frown. It… it sounds like a party. In my dining room.

When I walk into the dining room, I stop dead. There are dozens of women in there, all of them talking at once and holding wineglasses.

"Logan!" Callie crosses the room, grinning from ear to ear. "They all love the idea of the website."

This is about her website? "Who are they?" I ask.

As I glance around the room, I realize Callie wasn't joking about hiring the wives of everyone we know. There's a couple of VC wives, a CTO wife or two, and…

"Holy shit," I whisper into Callie's ear. "That can't be her."

"Who, Brienne?" She tries to spin to look, but I hold her back. "Yeah, she's here."

Brienne is the wife of Jack Collins, the CEO of Pixio, which is one of the biggest tech companies in the world. I know Jack and we're friends, but having his wife show up here is like having Michelle Obama show up. And Michelle Obama isn't going to be writing for any start-up media company no matter who's running it.

How the hell did Callie get her here? I never thought they were friends.

"Logan, you're home." Brienne is making a beeline for us. "Callie said you'd be late."

I'm guessing Jack's version of late is the same as mine, and eight o'clock isn't it.

"Got away early," I say with a tight smile since I'm really fucking confused here. "What's going on?"

"Callie told me all about her idea for a media company, and I love it. I want to write for her."

"You do?" All I really know about Brienne's work experience is that she's got some charity to put tablets in every school in America. "That's great."

"Oh, it will be. And I didn't even know…" She puts the tip of her tongue to her front teeth, calculating her next words. "I didn't even know Callie and I were fans of the same blog."

What blog? That's a weird thing to say. But maybe Brienne's just weird in general. "Oh? Which one?"

"*The Silicon Wife*." It's like she's waiting for me to react. "Do you know it?"

Next to me, Callie goes very stiff. But Brienne's not making me uncomfortable—I've been through too many awkward business parties to be put off by her.

"I haven't. I don't have much time to read blogs, I'm afraid."

Brienne laughs. "That's right, blogs are dead, as Jack keeps telling me."

"He would know," I say. "Pixio is always on top of what's next."

"Oh." Brienne's eyes go wide as someone across the room

catches her attention. "I've got to go talk to Autumn. If you'll excuse me."

When she's gone, I raise my eyebrows at Callie. "Brienne Collins writing for the site? That's going to be interesting."

"She has an MBA, you know," Callie says. I actually didn't know. "She's going to write under a pseudonym and not about anything to do with Pixio, but she follows the tech business really closely. I'm thinking a weekly column with her insights would be popular."

"Does Jack know?"

Callie takes a casual sip of her wine. "I think that's between the two of them, don't you? She doesn't have to get his permission."

"I never meant to suggest otherwise," I say with fake mildness. "How did you get in touch with her?"

"Like she said, we both read the same blog. She's a big commenter there, and I always like her comments."

I suppose stranger connections have been made over the internet before. "So these are all our writers, huh?"

"No, we'll have to hire some professional journalists too. And some of them are designers."

As I take in the crowd, I realize her friends are here too, the ones from before we married. Only a few of them bother to look back at me, and one raises her glass mockingly to me. Yeah, that's Gertrude, who when I last saw her, told me I was a gentrifying tech bro asshole.

Callie's friends never did like me.

"You gathered all these people together just today?" I ask.

A blush stains her cheeks. "I guess I was really excited about the site when I contacted them, and they got excited too."

I lean over and kiss her, softly, because the kiss I really want can wait until we're alone. "You're amazing."

"Wait until the site is actually built before you say that." But her hazel eyes glow with warmth.

"Nope." I kiss her again, deeper this time. "I'm going to say it now. And keep saying it." I kiss her one more time and keep my face close to hers. "How long until all these people go home?"

She finds my biceps and squeezes. "We can't just kick people out."

I give her a feral smile. "Watch me."

There's a dare teasing around the edges of her mouth, a dare I'm definitely going to take. I'm glad she and her friends love the idea of her site and are having fun, but I've got no reservations about ordering them out of my house and making it clear it's because I'm going to make love to my wife.

But before I can, Callie looks past me, her skin going pale. "Oh no. He can't be here."

The way she's says *he* immediately clues me into who it is. Anger burns hot under my skin. How dare that asshole come into my fucking house. Bad enough that he helped Callie run away, but to come into my *house*—

When I turn around, there Julian is, smirking like he's not expecting me to shove his teeth down his throat.

"Logan." Callie's voice is low and urgent, her hand on my arm holding me back. "He's my friend. Please don't."

*Fuck him.* The snarl is on my lips, my rage bleeding through my veins.

But Callie is there too, begging me with her gaze. Punching Julian, as satisfying as it would be, won't help Callie and me repair our marriage.

I shake out my shoulders, force my blood to cool. "I'll be... fine," I get out. I can't say cool or polite or well behaved because I won't be, but I won't embarrass her.

"Julian," she says, moving away from me. "How are you?"

Callie's smile is so warm and genuine my teeth grind.

Julian himself looks too good, like life is charmed.

*Do not punch that smug look off his face. Remember Callie and don't do it.*

My fist tightens anyway when Julian pulls Callie into his arms for a hug. I force my fingers open, one by one. Callie was friends with him way before she ever met me, and he's not here to steal her from me. He does, however, love to bait me.

I'm going to be the bigger man though. Or at least try.

Julian pulls away first, sets his hands on Callie's shoulders to study her. "You look happy." There's a hint of an accusation there.

Fuck it. I'm not going to be too well behaved. I reach for Callie's elbow, pull her back, and set my arm across her shoulders. "Doesn't she though?"

"I'm feeling… better," Callie says. There's an edge to her voice.

I tighten my arm around her.

"Good." Julian's still studying her, having ignored my comment. "I saw the story in *TidBytes* yesterday, and I was worried. And then you didn't answer your phone…" His gaze swings to me.

"In the shop," I explain. "For repairs." I don't mention the replacement phone I got her, because his number definitely wasn't programmed into it.

"Well, thank goodness she managed to get ahold of me today." Julian's smile would fit right on a shark's face. "Otherwise I would have missed this."

"That would have been just too bad." I make my smile as sharp as his.

Callie reaches over and pinches my stomach. Hard. "I'm right here, and I know what you two are doing."

"We're just talking," Julian says.

"You're not, and it's upsetting me," Callie says flatly.

Shit. As enjoyable as it is to fuck with Julian, even a little bit, I don't want to upset Callie. "I'll be nice from now on. I promise."

Julian remains pointedly silent.

Well, screw him. I can be the bigger man here—after all, I'm the one who's married to Callie. And he's just *a friend*.

## CHAPTER 18

I'm happy to see Julian—I really am—I only wish he'd come any other time.

I knew he'd be here once I texted him I was back in the City. Cute move of Logan's, not to put Julian's number in the new phone, but I've memorized it.

And now he and Logan are squaring off like they're about to knock each other out.

Julian pulls his phone out of his pocket. "I don't mean to upset you," he says to me. "But have you seen this? *TidBytes* just put up a new story, late edition. Callie, leaving your office"—his gaze swings to Logan like a blade—"her hand over face like she's been crying. And the headline is WHAT HAPPENS WHEN YOU LEAVE A BASTARD."

Oh God. I should have expected something like that. "Let me see." I haven't even checked *TidBytes* today—I was too busy sketching, and then there was the partners' meeting and arranging this get-together. It didn't occur to me to look at it.

Julian hands over his phone, and sure enough, there's me in my oversized sweater, my hands covering my face like I'm sobbing into them.

"That's not from today." I looked powerful, put together

when I went into the office today. But yesterday... "I wasn't crying. I swear I wasn't crying."

"You don't have to convince me," Julian says gently.

"It was..." I take a deep inhale. "It was tense, yes, but I wasn't crying."

Logan's arm tightens around me, but he says nothing. I can't tell if he believes me or not.

"Okay," Julian says slowly.

I pull myself out from under Logan's arm. "I need to talk to him somewhere less loud. Okay?"

I'm not asking him for permission; I'm asking him to understand. He's never been easy around Julian, and I know it's gotten worse since I left.

Finally, his jaw tense, he nods. "I'll entertain here."

My shoulders slump down as the muscles release. Thank goodness; Logan will play the perfect host while I'm gone, which hopefully will keep the gossip down.

There will be talk—I can already see the speculation in some eyes as they watch the three of us. At least there won't be any damn pictures of it on *TidBytes* tomorrow.

Julian and I end up in my office. "Nice," he says as he takes it in. "Great view."

"The divorce isn't happening," I say bluntly. "Logan brought the papers but... but somehow *TidBytes* found out. They had the story yesterday"—God, did all that happen just *yesterday*?—"and Minerva Dyne came to my house to offer to buy my shares in the divorce. For Corvus."

"Corvus?" Julian looks like I've just smashed a pie in his face. "Fuchs offered for your shares?"

"I technically don't have any shares because I'm not getting divorced," I say pointedly. "It turns out that Fuchs owns *TidBytes*. All those..." I swallow hard, because it still hurts to remember. "All those stories—he was behind them."

"Who told you that?" Julian's voice is dangerously quiet.

"Logan. His brother found out—"

"Jesus, Callie, don't fall for his bullshit again! You know he's not gonna change. Not about work and not about the women. You've seen for yourself."

"He said..." I believe Logan, I really do, but it hurts. I don't want to think about it. "He said he never cheated. He's not lying."

"Oh, well, great for him." Julian starts to pace. "Gold star for his chore list. But what about never being home? What about caring more about Bastard Capital than you?"

I can't answer any of that. But I also can't give up on us, not yet. And not just because I've got a deal with Logan.

"He was home early tonight." I can't even describe how happy I was to see him. "And we're doing this website together."

Julian stops when he catches sight of my expression. "I'm sorry, it's just... It wasn't just the *TidBytes* stuff, remember?"

"Of course I do. But Fuchs did try to ruin my marriage. I can't let that go. And I can't let him do that to anyone else."

Julian sinks down into an easy chair, sprawling so he takes up every inch. "The site is a good idea. I don't know that going back to Logan was."

"I still love him." I'm not ready to tell Logan that, but I can trust Julian with it. "If we can make it work this time, I have to try."

Julian stares at me for a long moment, then shrugs one shoulder. "I'll be here for whatever you need then."

I know he will, because he was there for me when I had to leave. Not many men would have risked Logan's wrath to help me.

"Thanks." I reach out and squeeze his hand briefly.

"What does your mother say?"

"I haven't told her yet. She was the one who told Logan

where I was, after he told her he'd drawn up the divorce papers."

Facing my mother was going to be much, much harder than facing down the Bastards. I know she only wants what's best for me, but her idea of *best* and mine diverged a long time ago.

"Well, no matter what she says, just remember that she really does love you."

"Yeah." I pull at the sleeves of my shirt, forgetting that I'm not wearing my sweater and I can't hide my hands. "It'll be fine."

Julian rises out of the chair in one fluid motion. If I weren't so in love with Logan, I might appreciate it more. But I can only look at Julian with an artist's eye.

"We should head back before your husband hunts me down for stealing you again."

I roll my eyes but walk to the door anyway. "You didn't steal me."

"That's not what he thinks."

Julian walks down the hall, past the living room where the party's still going, and gives me a wave. "I'm taking off. Tell Logan I said bye."

I shake my head affectionately. "No, I won't. You know how he reacts to you."

"Seriously." For a moment Julian stops being my friend and becomes Julian the businessman. "You need anything for the site, come to me. Whoever your husband can't put you in contact with, I probably can."

"Thanks." I give him a quick hug. "You're always there when I need you."

It's to Julian's credit that he doesn't say anything about Logan not being there when I needed him.

Which is good, because right then Logan walks into the hall. "All done chatting?"

I don't know how a voice so smooth can be so menacing.

"We are." I give him a defiant look. "Julian wanted to hear all about the site."

"And make sure Callie was doing fine." Julian aims that at Logan.

"She's my wife. You don't have to worry about her. In fact, I suggest you don't."

So much for Logan playing nice. Although I have to admit, he's toned down some of the aggressive masculinity he was playing on earlier.

"I've always worried about her, even before you got married." Julian is dead serious now—he's not saying this to rattle Logan. "The usual wife stuff around here... it's not her."

"*Not her*?" Logan flicks out a hand. "She never has to worry about money ever again. How is that somehow suffocating her?"

Julian shakes his head. "Good luck," he says to me. And then he's gone.

I turn to Logan, both hands on my hips, and wait.

"What?" he says, like he's done nothing wrong.

"Go ahead. Tell me he can't come again."

"I'd never say that. He's your friend."

My mouth tightens. Logan's not giving me the fight I was expecting. "But you don't believe that."

"It's hard to," he says with bland silkiness, "when he enjoys getting in my face so much. Even you have to have noticed it."

Guilt snaps through me because I have. Sometimes Julian's insistence on my getting free of Logan felt too personal in an icky way. Not that Julian wanted me for himself but to get one over on Logan.

"He's still my friend." My defiance is leaking away though, because it's hard to argue with someone who's so determined not to.

"And you should invite all your friends. In fact, you should have over anyone you want." He leans close, the scent of him filling my senses. His aftershave is faint now, threaded through the stronger scent of his skin.

My mouth goes dry because I want to lick him so badly.

"Just remember," Logan says, the menace back. But it's a good menace, the kind that makes heat pool between my legs. "Julian might be your friend, but I'm your husband."

He runs his hand along my exposed collarbone, claiming the skin he and only he has the right to touch. My knees go weak, and a little moan leaves my throat.

One corner of Logan's mouth twitches. He's won.

I want to be annoyed with him, but he's so goddamn hot when he's triumphant. Whether it's successfully launching a company or cashing in on a risky investment—or winning a ridiculous pissing match—he wears his wins with a compelling confidence. It makes me want to launch myself at him.

I'd want to punch him first, yes, but then I'd kiss him. And I'd put a lot more effort into the kiss than the punch.

## CHAPTER 19

I'm walking into the office late, but I don't care.

All right, maybe I care a little, especially with the looks the associates are giving me, but it was too damn hard to leave Callie this morning. She was eating one of the chocolate-covered strawberries for breakfast and moaning like she was orgasming, so I pulled her onto the couch and gave her the real thing.

Which meant I left an hour later than I meant to and got stuck in traffic on the 280, and now I'm walking up to my office door two hours later than I wanted.

But the sex *was* incredible.

"What the fuck?"

Okay, maybe not the best thing for me to say first thing when I come in to work, but there's yellow caution tape strung all across my office door. I can't even open it without breaking the tape.

"Finn, is this one of your stunts?"

Finn loves to pull elaborate pranks, like reversing all the furniture in Paul's office and rewiring all the light switches in Mark's office so that they control the fixtures in Elliot's office. We put up with it because he's fucking genius.

Finn pops his head out of his office. "Nope. Not this time. Anjie put up the tape. Ask her."

When I find her, Anjie's sitting at her desk, innocent as can be. Well, she looks like she ought to be winking at you from the nose of a World War II bomber, so not *that* innocent.

"What happened with my office?" I ask.

Her expression is so bland it worries me. "The sink in your bathroom started leaking last night. And went *all* night. The carpet's ruined, along with the cabinets and part of one wall. It's going to take weeks to fix."

I can't shake the feeling that she's lying, but why would she lie about that? But there's something about the set of her eyes that has my instincts perking up.

A workman dressed in blue and carrying a heavy toolbox walks past us, waving to Anjie as he does. If she's faking, she's gone to a ton of work on it.

"Okay," I say slowly, "I'll take one of the intern offices then. Put them in the little conference room."

"Oooh." Her eyebrows twist apologetically. "We can't do that, because their employment contract states they have to have a designated office."

"We have a contract with them? What the fuck, are they unionized or something?"

How the hell are the interns guaranteed an office and I'm not?

Anjie tries to look sympathetic but doesn't quite make it. "You could work from home. Isn't telecommuting the future?"

I spear her with a look. "If you're thinking about not coming in anymore…"

When we say we'd fall apart without Anjie, we're not joking. If she wasn't here, reining us in, this place would become a frat house. God only knows what Finn would do to the wiring then.

She grins. "Of course not. I'd miss you guys too much."

I stare at her longer. She stares back.

"So that's it?" I ask. "I just get kicked out and have to work from home?"

My tone is casual, but my nerves aren't. I *need* to be here, focused solely on my work.

"Look, it's only for a few weeks," Anjie says. "I'll send over everything you need, hire a temp for your assistant, and check on you every day. I was going to send someone over to your house to help Callie anyway."

*Callie.* Talk about distractions. She's at home, waiting for me. Working, too, on our project but also waiting for me.

Something inside me settles at the thought.

"I guess it makes sense," I say slowly. "Since I have to consult with Callie on this."

Anjie smiles like I'm the slow kid who's finally gotten an answer right. "My exact thoughts. If we have to redo your office, now is the perfect time."

"Great." Somehow I've been manipulated here, but I can't quite see how. Anjie wouldn't destroy my office just for kicks, would she?

No, of course not. Fuchs has made me too paranoid.

I head for the door. "I'll let you clean out my office and send everything over." I stop suddenly. "I'm not going to have to pick out carpet samples or anything, am I?"

Anjie makes a shooing motion. "Of course not. I'll handle everything."

When she says *everything*, I get the sense she means my marriage too.

The drive up the peninsula is much quicker than the drive down, and I'm pulling into my own driveway in under an hour.

Callie isn't even surprised to see me when I walk into her office. "Oh, there you are."

"You knew I was coming?" Like I've said, I hate being two steps behind.

"Anjie called me about your office. I told her what colors to redecorate in."

I'm caught up short. That's so... wifely. And she didn't even hesitate to do it.

"Thanks." I clear my throat because it's only some stupid paint colors. "Anjie's going to send my stuff over later, along with an assistant for us."

That perks her up. "I get an assistant?"

"Of course. You're going to need one." I look around her office. I could work in the room we call the study—leather chairs, lots of books, but hardly every used—or maybe the dining room.

Funny thing is, I don't have an office at home. I made sure Callie's office was everything she could ever ask for but didn't make an office for myself. I told myself it was because I worked better at Bastard Capital... but I was also worried Callie would distract me here.

She's so very distracting.

She's watching me now, her eyes wide and guileless. Her lips are wet—she must have just licked them—and I can't think of anything but kissing her.

Fuck.

"I need to set up a workspace," I say too curtly.

Callie raises her eyebrows. "We could share this office."

Oh hell no. If I'm worried about her distracting me when we're in the same building, being in the same room is not an improvement.

She's waiting for me to say no. I can see the doubt in the crinkles around her eyes, the tension at the corners of her mouth.

"The printer's here," she says, "and the router, and the desk is built for two."

She's right about all of it. If I wanted to not be an asshole, I'd just say yes.

"I don't want to disturb you." But that's a stupid excuse, because Callie's never had a problem with my looking over her shoulder when she's working. In fact, she invites it.

"You won't." She turns back to her screen as if she doesn't care what I do. But her fingers tremble as she picks her stylus back up.

"If you're sure." I sit down across from her, at the empty side of the desk. She's half blocked by her monitor, but even that small slice of her profile is lovely beyond words.

She doesn't look away from her work, although her shoulders relax. "There's coffee in the pot."

I frown at it. "We haven't gotten you a new machine yet?"

"That one's fine."

I grab my phone and text Anjie. "Anjie'll bring a new machine when she comes."

"Anything else that doesn't meet with your approval?" Her tone is dry, dry enough to make me smile.

"Yeah. We need automatic shades in here so the light is always right for you. And you're wearing gloves—the heat needs to be turned up. What about lunch? Did you order something already?"

Her tongue is stuck firmly in her cheek, and I can tell she's trying hard not to laugh. "I was going to make a sandwich. And I'm warm enough, but for some reason my fingers are always cold. I'm used to the gloves."

I could take her hands in mine and rub some warmth into her fingers. They're long and graceful, although I can only see the very tips with the fingerless gloves she's wearing. Callie used to paint her nails the wildest colors, with all kinds of art on them, but her nails are bare now.

She's wearing that awful sweater again. I know I shouldn't care, but watching her wrap herself in it like she wants to disappear makes my jaw clench. Is she cold? Frightened? Nervous?

None of those are how she should be.

"Hypatia," I call out.

"Yes?"

"Turn up the heat. To seventy-four degrees."

"Of course."

Callie's got a hand over her mouth, and she's definitely laughing now. I don't care as long as she warms up.

"Thank you," she says with exaggerated care.

I nod, then pull out my own laptop. I try to concentrate, but she's too close. I can hear her breath, slow and gentle, and smell her soap, and I'm dying to know what she's working on.

"What are you doing today?" I ask without looking up from my screen.

"Some more logo treatments. Brienne and I are going to look at the office space this afternoon."

I know she's going to hate this, but Brienne Collins writing for the site in secret is a terrible idea. It's like planting a fucking time bomb right in the middle of the site, ready to destroy everything once someone finds out.

"I still think she needs to tell Jack before she does this." I don't look up from my screen, and not because I'm afraid of Callie's reaction. There's an important email here I need to reply to.

"Brienne wants to do it, and she's a grown woman."

"I know that, but he's my colleague and my friend. If he came to you with something like this, without my knowing, I'd be pissed. How long until someone figures out it's her and it gets back to him? I mean, let's just *talk* to Elliot about the legal implications."

I don't think I'm being unreasonable here, but Callie goes very, very still.

Shit. I fucking dread having to ask this, but I can't let it go any longer. Not with how she reacts every time to any mention of Elliot. "Did something happen between you and him?"

Elliot's difficult to love. He's rigid and too logical and unfriendly, so it's easy for people to misread him. Or not— sometimes when he offends you, he means to. But there's something deeper going on than just Elliot being Elliot.

"Nothing happened," Callie says. She's picking out her words too carefully. "I mean, he hardly talks to me."

"They why do you freeze up whenever I mention him?"

She keeps sketching with the stylus, but her movements are slow as if she's moving through syrup. "He hates me. That's why. I've never done anything to him—except marry you—and he hates me. He's your brother, and he hates me."

"Elliot? Elliot doesn't hate anyone." That's not exactly true —he'd like to throttle Fuchs's assistant, but she insulted his lawyerly prowess. Callie hasn't done that.

"He hates me. Every time he looks at me, I feel like I'm going to catch on fire."

Suddenly it occurs to me that we've never really talked about Elliot. When we first got together, it was so intense there wasn't room for anyone else, not even family.

"He looks at everyone like that. Elliot doesn't have an off switch. Or even a dimmer. He was probably thinking about some contract or some case. Hell, he looks at me like that, but I know he's not mad."

She rubs her arms. "It feels personal. He wanted you to divorce me, didn't he?" That last line is very quiet.

"Elliot doesn't linger. When you left... He wanted me to move on. He thought it would be best for me."

"Has he ever had a relationship?"

Oh fuck. How to answer that one? "He, uh, has some intimate partners."

A stupid way to say it, but I couldn't say "fuck buddy" to her. Elliot isn't exactly smooth, but somehow women flock to him. Maybe it's the challenge of him. I've never met any of his partners, not formally, but I've seen him leave plenty of parties with a lady on his arm.

Callie raises one eyebrow. "Intimate partners?" She holds up a finger. "No, I get it. So what happened with Mark and January? And who is she exactly? You never really said."

"For Mark, she's the one who got away. She came to us looking for funding for her start-up, which Fuchs wanted. Turned out he'd kidnapped her roommate, and January was next on his list."

Her eyes go wide and she sets down her graphics tablet with a snap. "What?"

That's exactly how I reacted when I first heard. "Fuchs had put spyware on smartphones, snuck it in through all kinds of apps. Her roommate was working on it for him, and January built a program to stop him. That's why I had Elliot give your phone to her."

Her skin is a shade of green that makes my gut clench. "That's… unbelievable." Her voice is weak, faded.

"It all worked out." I make my own voice firm, strong. She has nothing to worry about. "His spyware program is dead, her roommate doesn't work there anymore, and Mark and January got together."

"Wow." Some color comes back into her cheeks. "I missed a lot."

I raise my eyebrows in a shrug. "Never a dull moment."

I keep my tone casual because Callie doesn't need to worry about that, but I can't help but think of how Fuchs must have plans to take the rest of the Bastards down. Or at least try to.

"That's a lot bigger than just running a gossip blog," Callie says finally. There's doubt in her beautiful eyes.

"Not to me." My jaw tightens. "You left me because of it."

If I could go back, erase every last one of those awful pictures, I would. But I can't, so I'm going to ruin that fucking blog instead.

Her mouth turns down. "Not just because of that."

I don't want to argue with her, not today. I want to enjoy being with her. So I change the subject.

"Did you find any writers besides Brienne?"

For a moment it looks like she doesn't want to shift to that, but eventually she says, "I found a bunch of people on Twitter and pulled up their résumés."

I walk around the desk to peer over her shoulder at them. "Greg Tychie is good. I liked his stuff about the wider implications of a Bitcoin crash. And so is Lila Johnston."

"She and Greg are together," Callie says.

"They are? Why didn't I know that?" I'm the details guy. I don't like missing important ones.

She cranes her neck to look back at me. "Logan, it's not something you could figure out from studying their résumés for hours. Or their articles."

"So how do you know?"

Her cheeks go pink. "I stalked their Twitters. They always like each other's Tweets, even the pictures of their lunches, and they share in-jokes. Also, they're both in LA now, while Greg was in New York just a few months ago. I think he moved for her."

The dreamy quality to Callie's voice makes me frown. "Maybe he got a job in LA and they got together after he moved."

"They were couple-y on Twitter before he moved. And he's freelancing now—I don't think the journalism market in LA is that great."

That's… that's not something I could ever do. Just get up and move, without knowing I had a job waiting for me. Not that it matters since I have more money than I'll ever need, but it's the principle of the thing.

But hell, it's not my life. If Greg wants to act like a damn fool, it's nothing to me. I'd just never do it.

"We should go down to LA to talk to them. Take the jet, make it a weekend."

Callie raised an eyebrow. "You mean take a weekend off?"

"You're cute when you try to be stealthy." I run the back of my hand down her cheek because her skin is driving me crazy this close. I have to touch. "It's not a weekend off if we're doing work too."

"But not all work? Some play?"

I run my fingers down to her neck, sliding them under the cowl of her sweater. Her eyes darken.

"Definitely some play." I lean into her ear. "Maybe a lot of play."

"Mmm." Her head falls to the side, giving me access to her neck. "I like the sound of that."

I do too, but I want to play *now*. I want to carry her off to my bed and spend hours losing myself in her.

I take her earlobe in my teeth, flicking it with my tongue. She releases a luxurious moan, lifting a hand to reach for my arm.

I kiss my way down to her neck, snagging the neck of her sweater with a hooked finger and dragging it down. I can't wait to pull this sweater off her and see the beautiful curves it's hiding—

My laptop pings. On instinct, I snap up. That's our Slack channel—someone's messaged me.

Shit. And here I was, getting distracted by Callie. This is exactly what I was worried about.

Callie's breathing is quick, shallow, but her cheeks have gone pale. She's not pleased we've been interrupted.

I could ignore the message, shut my laptop, and still carry her off to bed.

But I won't. I'm not that kind of man.

"I have to check that."

She nods once, sharply. "Sure. And I need to go meet Brienne and see our new office space."

Callie leaves without even a goodbye.

I sigh as I pull up our Slack channel. Okay, she's pissed, but I can't ignore a message from the office. And I really do need to get back to work.

I'll make it up to her tonight once I can give her my full attention. Work needs it right now though.

# CHAPTER 20

I've been in office spaces before, plenty of times. But they usually weren't empty. And I was never the one expected to fill them.

"This place is great." Brienne might be more excited about this entire thing than I am. She can't stop talking about the space, the concept, and finally doing something *real* again.

Her charities are pretty real, especially to the people they help, but I don't think that's what she means.

"It's nice," I agree. Or at least it will be once we have some furniture and people in it. "I've got a friend who'll do the interior. She'll start tomorrow."

"That's right." Brienne snaps her fingers. "You used to be an artist."

"Graphic designer," I say gently. I don't say anything about how I still *am* a designer even if I haven't been working recently.

"And now you're starting a news site." Brienne lifts her eyebrows. "How did that happen?" She shakes her head. "No, wait. Explain to me how you're the Silicon Wife. I still can't believe it."

I still can't believe that Brienne is KatinaKat, the commenter whom I suspected of having an MBA. I reached out to some of the blog commenters yesterday, anonymously, mentioning that I might have a writing opportunity for them. Brienne was the only one who wrote back.

To say that I was shocked when I found out who she really was would be putting it mildly. I was probably as shocked as *she* was when she found out who I was.

"I needed someplace to put my thoughts," I say simply. "So I started the blog. The name was a joke, and I never expected anyone to read it."

"Then why not buy a journal?"

She has a point. Maybe subconsciously, I did want people to hear me. People like her, who would understand.

I smile. "I'll do that next time."

"No." Brienne's eyes widen. "Don't do that. I love *The Silicon Wife*. It says all the things I want to but can't."

My heart warms to hear it, but I have to disappoint her. "There's no way I keep on with the blog. Nobody knows I write it. Except for you."

"Really?" She leans in, sharing a secret. "But then how did *TidBytes* know about the divorce?"

Answering that would take too long and give away too many things I have to keep secret. "It wasn't from my blog," I say quickly. "And I'm not getting a divorce."

I shift my weight, wishing I'd worn lower heels. These shoes are gorgeous, but my feet haven't toughened up yet. They're still used to going barefoot.

"Hmm." Something changes in her expression. "Logan doesn't know you write the blog?" she asks carefully.

Oh boy. This is not a subject I want to get into. My feet throb as I say, "It was just a hobby. And now we're building this site together, so I don't need it anymore."

Her eyes narrow. "You disappeared for months." I can see

the whip-smart intelligence now. "Left him without a word, according to all the rumors. But everything's fine suddenly?"

"We're reconciling, yes." I keep my expression and voice upbeat, steady. Brienne doesn't need to know the ugly details of my marriage.

"Well." She rocks back on her heels. "I thought you'd finally got the nerve up to leave him and make it permanent."

My mouth drops open. "Excuse me?"

She gives an elegant snort. "Have you seen the pictures in *TidBytes*? Of course you have. No one knew anything concrete about him cheating, but where there's smoke, there's fire, right?"

That's exactly what I used to think. And it seems that's what everyone else in the tech world thinks about our marriage.

Fuchs's scorched-earth campaign has burned more than I knew.

"Do you know who owns *TidBytes*?" I ask.

"New Media Holdings, a subsidy of Pelanos Corporation," she rattles off without a beat.

I'm impressed she knows that much. She really does follow the business side closely. But she doesn't know everything.

"No, who *really* owns *TidBytes*," I say. "The owner of the hand holding that shell corporation."

"Who?"

I hesitate for a brief moment. If I spread this information around, Fuchs could come after me again. I take a deep breath and blurt out, "Arne Fuchs."

"What?" People must have heard her screech from two floors away. "But he's got Corvus to run and all those other companies he's invested in... Why would he care about a gossipy news site?"

"Think about all the pictures of Logan. Think about what they did to my marriage."

Her expression shifts like sunlight on water, revealing hidden depths. "Shit. There was a story on Jack recently. Nothing explicitly libelous, but still… it didn't sit well with him. Or me."

"Yeah, I know the feeling." We share a smile—small, wistful. "Technology is great, but what better way to manipulate people than through gossip? Humanity's been doing it for millennia now."

"I'm actually surprised Fuchs came up with the scheme. He doesn't really seem the type."

I start as I realize—she's probably met Fuchs. Tons of times. Shaken hands with him, made small talk, and all the while he's been pulling this BS.

"Well," I say carefully, "based on what Logan has been telling me, I think Fuchs is the type to do anything to gain power. And if that means buying up companies or breaking up marriages, that's what he'll do."

She sends me a shrewd, penetrating look. "But he *didn't* break up your marriage."

"It's complicated." I almost laugh at myself because it's so much more than complicated and to hide the hurt that bubbles up. "It's hard to have a marriage when you never see your husband. The pictures in *TidBytes* weren't the only reason I left, but they didn't help."

Brienne holds my gaze, sympathy softening her face. She nods. "Oh yes. When the kids were little, Jack was never home. It was just me and them, morning, noon, and night. I kept thinking that once he got that next promotion, that next raise, that next position, we'd be secure enough for him to slow down. But these guys don't work that way. It's not about the money. It's about the hustle."

I shiver even though the building is perfectly climate

controlled. If she's right, if Logan can never slow down, then we'll be right back where we started. With me miserable and alone, and him at work, completely oblivious.

"You have your charities," I offer. That's our prize for marrying so well—we get to do so much good in the world.

She laughs without humor. "Oh yeah. And really, we do a ton of good work. But sometimes it feels like a toy Jack's given me. Like we have all this money—he makes it and I play with it." Her smile twists bitterly. "I sound like such an ungrateful bitch. Here we've got so much, enough to change the world with our foundation, and I'm complaining about it."

If she's an ungrateful bitch, then I'm something even worse. But to hear someone else say all that, out loud instead of in a comment on my anonymous blog post, feels... amazing. Like I'm not quite as alone as I thought.

"I know what you mean," I say. "We're all forced into that mold, aren't we? We can't work—then we're taking a job from someone who needs it. And of course we have to do something good with our wealth, but... it's complicated."

Brienne laughs again, this time closer to her usual laugh. "Exactly. But enough rich-lady complaining." She claps her hands, her glee echoing through the empty space. "Let's get back to this exciting new venture of yours."

"Can I help?" A stylish woman with ink-black hair pops her head in. Something about her is familiar, but I can't quite place her.

Something about her is unsettling too, like she's part of a bad memory or something.

"Sorry, maybe you don't remember me." She holds out her hand to me. "I'm January. My office is just around the way, and I thought I'd stop by and introduce myself. Offer any help you might need."

Suddenly I remember—she was with Mark when he

confronted Julian and me at the private club. God, that was so humiliating.

"I'm Callie." I'm praying she doesn't remember that, but of course she must. But if she's willing to pretend that never happened, then so am I. "It's nice to finally meet you. Officially, that is." I gesture to Brienne. "And this is Brienne."

January must recognize her, but she gives no sign of it as she shakes Brienne's hand. "So nice to meet you too."

"Same. Look, I'd love to chat," Brienne says with an apologetic smile, "but I need to run. My masseuse threatened to fire me if I was late one more time, and she's got the most magical hands."

Once she's gone, there's a beat of awkwardness between January and me. Mark can't have told her anything good about me.

But she still sought me out and said hello. Maybe she wants to draw her own conclusions.

"Mark told me about what you were doing," she says finally. "I think it's great. Fuchs is such a bastard."

A knot in my stomach unravels. "Yeah, he is." I let my shoulders relax. "Logan told me what Fuchs did to you. Are you okay?"

January smiles like she finds my concern funny, but in a friendly way. "Everything turned out fine in the end. And Mark and I got together, so…" Her grin turns wicked. "If I were a nicer person, I'd be thanking Fuchs for that."

I think I'm going to like this woman very much. "I'm sure you would have found each other even without Fuchs. And really, nobody deserves some meanness more than him."

January nods. Her skin is pale, and her hair is so black she looks like someone out of a fairy tale. But the spark in her eye tells me she doesn't need any rescuing. "Oh, trust me, I hope you give him a heart attack with this website. Fuchs tried to attack my company, and he's trying to get my friend deported—if there's anything I can do to help, I'll do it. I'm deadly serious."

I blink, feeling foolish for being so overwhelmed with emotion. Last night, all those people came to support *me* and all at the drop of a hat, while today both Brienne and January have offered their support.

And Logan's at home, waiting for me. It's almost too much.

"Thanks," I say in a strained voice, trying not to let all that emotion out. "I really appreciate it."

"Logan is Mark's friend. They're like brothers, which makes us... maybe not sisters. How about cousins?"

As she says that, the awkwardness comes rushing back in. January doesn't know anything about why I left, and I can tell from her expression she feels like she put her foot in it.

"Or not," she says quickly. "Mark didn't have all the details of your reconciliation. Or whatever it might be."

Her skin is going pink, probably as pink as mine is turning.

Oh, this is silly. I'm trying to be nice, she's trying to be nice, and we're both tiptoeing around the horrible, awful incident we were both involved in. Might as well face the unspoken thing head-on.

"Look," I say, "about what happened with Mark and Julian—"

January stops me there. "Don't even worry about it. Mark is wonderful and I love him, but he's also..." She shrugs and then grins. "Well, he's a Bastard. You're married to one, so you know all about it."

"Yes, those guys are definitely intense." I don't smile, because I don't find the rest of them as charming as January does. "And Julian doesn't bring out the best in them."

January hooks her arm in mine. "But you're friends with him, and it sounds like he helped you when you needed it. Anyone who can set those guys off must be intriguing." Her expression is a study in delighted mischief. "Want to grab coffee and tell me all about it?"

## CHAPTER 21

"What do you think the two of them did all day?"

Mark doesn't look up at my question, keeping his attention on the three fingers of scotch the waiter has brought over. "I don't know." He's clearly not as concerned as I am.

The bar we're in is at the top of a forty-story hotel, with a view of Union Square to our left and the rise of Nob Hill before us. There are no tourists here since this place isn't open to the public. It's only for exclusive guests of the hotel. Very exclusive guests.

Mark used to stay here regularly, back when he was having one-night stands on the regular. Now that he's with January, that's all done, but it looks like he's kept the other perks of his account here.

"What did January say?" I ask.

"That she and Callie were out together and we should meet them for drinks and dinner." Mark stretches out his legs.

"And she left the office at noon?"

Mark and January share an office at her company more days than not. I'm sharing an office with my wife, but I hardly saw her at all today. She was out with January, doing I don't know what.

The house felt incredibly empty without Callie there.

"Left at noon, said she was going to say hi to Callie, and didn't come back." He takes a sip of his whiskey. "What, are you afraid they spent the whole time shit talking you?"

He doesn't have to look so goddamn smug. "If they're shit talking me, they're shit talking you too, genius."

Mark snorts. "No way. January thinks I'm perfect."

Now I snort. "Oh yeah? I'll tell her you said that."

"Oooh. Someone's pissy because they can't use their office."

"That's not—" I take a slug of my own scotch, because yeah, maybe I am a little on edge. "It was fine."

It wasn't. I got plenty of work done, sure, but I felt like I forgot something or left it behind at the office. And I couldn't figure out what the fuck it was.

I also couldn't stop thinking about Callie's insistence that I worked too much. I didn't, but I was home all day today and she wasn't there. She was going to be my one consolation for being exiled from my office, and she took off.

Of course, I was also worried she was going to distract me. And then she wasn't even there to do it.

I take another long drink, the scotch setting my throat on fire. I need to get back into my office and get my mind right again.

Then Callie walks in, and I'm tipped upside down all over again.

"Oh shit."

When Callie and January come across the room toward Mark and me, their heads so close they look glued together, it's all I can think to say. They both gleam among everyone else in this room. If I'd never seen Callie before this, I still wouldn't be able to take my eyes off her. The long fall of her hair, the lean elegance of her body, the light in her eyes all make her irresistible.

The twist of Callie's mouth says she's got mischief planned. January is wearing the same expression.

"That looks… not good," Mark says. "What do you think they're talking about?"

"Us. Of course. And they're laughing."

January catches sight of us, wriggles her fingers in greeting, then whispers something to Callie, which makes Callie dissolve into laughter.

"What did she say?" I ask Mark out of the side of my mouth.

"Probably some embarrassing secret about me. Or a joke about you. Or both."

"They've united against us."

"Yeah," Mark says, his smile widening. "Isn't it great?"

I don't have time to answer him because Callie and January arrive at our table. Mark and I both stand up because women that beautiful deserve a tribute.

"What were you two up to today?" Mark asks.

January kisses him, then smiles. "Coffee. And shopping. Callie has the best taste in shoes."

"I hope you bought the store out," Mark says.

"Ha. Wait until I take over your closet."

"I'll just build you another one," Mark murmurs.

The affection between them is so strong it makes my heart ping with wistfulness. Callie and I used to tease like that. But right now I'm not thinking about teasing her.

She's been gone all day, and I've been going crazy all alone in the house, smelling her perfume in the air, finding her things scattered around but not having her to grasp.

If we weren't with one of my best friends and his girlfriend, I'd drag her to a hotel room and show her how crazy.

"I missed you" is all I say right before I kiss her. Her eyes widen like she wasn't expecting that, but she kisses me back, first with gentle hesitation, then with more urgency.

I break it off before I lose my head even more.

When I help Callie to her seat, I lean in to breathe in her scent. There's her perfume, light with a hint of flowers and something grassy, but beneath is her. I brush my nose against her neck, too quick for anyone else to see, but enough to get a deeper whiff of her.

Her lips part on a short gasp, her cheeks darkening. There's no woman half as gorgeous as her here, no woman even a one hundredth as sexy. She's the single blooming blood-red rose among them, and they're only tiny white flowers included to set off her beauty.

"Did you miss me?" I ask, dark and low. I already know the answer, but I want to hear it.

She turns her head, her hair brushing my cheek. "Of course."

I want to wrap my fingers in her hair, tilt her face up to mine, and kiss her until we're both drunk with it. Instead, I take my chair, letting my legs fall apart so that my knee is against hers.

That's my space there, and I'm going to take it.

"Callie's office is right next to mine," January says. "I'm so excited to have her right around the corner."

"What did you think of it?" I ask.

Callie blinks and tears her gaze away from me. I can't be certain, but I think she was staring at my mouth. "Um… it was great." She focuses on Mark and January. "And the neighbors are friendly."

They laugh, and that starts off an entire conversation about the new office and how to set it up.

I don't give a damn about the office except that Callie is happy with it. Instead, I watch my wife, how her hand curls around the base of her throat as she talks, the easy grace in her arms as she takes her drink from the waiter, the flash of her eyes as she laughs.

Something inside my chest, dark and crouching, eases at the sight. When she's with me, I feel... freer. Like I can stretch my soul and let it relax.

Things in my life have been unbearably cramped since she left, my world too small for me to move around in.

"...and we wanted to ask what you think, Logan?"

January's been talking the entire time, batting words around with Mark, but I haven't heard a thing she's said. And I'm supposed to be the details guy.

I take up my scotch and salute her and Callie. "I think Mark and I are the luckiest Bastards in this bar, thanks to you ladies."

Mark drapes his arm over January's chair, then loudly whispers, "He wasn't paying attention."

There's a wicked spark in January's eye. "Yes, he was. He was paying attention to Callie."

A glorious blush sneaks up Callie's neck, painting her skin in pink. Her bottom lip disappears between her teeth, and I want to bite that exact spot myself.

"Can you blame me?" I ask. I press a kiss to the back of Callie's hand. Again, the scent of her skin fills me, and my pulse leaps.

We *are* in a hotel. I could carry her out of here, demand the penthouse suite for the night, and fuck her until we pass out.

She's thinking the same thing—her dark eyes, deep inhales, and sudden stillness tell me exactly what's on her mind.

Mark wouldn't mind if we excuse ourselves, but January and Callie probably would. Women like this double date crap.

January tucks her chin into her palm. "Aww. That's so sweet."

"I'm sweet," Mark says with mock hurt.

"Actually, you're not." The way January looks at him says that she likes him that way.

"Now who's being sappy?" Callie asks. Her smile is small but true, and it hits me—she's enjoying this.

I am too. Yes, I want to drag her to the nearest bed as soon as I can, but enjoying her in this setting is a good second choice.

"Mark's allergic to sappy." January's eyes twinkle.

"Not true," he counters. "I got you that ridiculous over-stuffed bear you wanted last weekend. The pink one that was holding a heart."

"And broke out into a rash when you did."

"So that's what was on your ass," I say.

A laugh bursts out from Callie. She looks shocked that she did that. "Why were you looking at his butt?"

"Have you *seen* my butt?" Mark says. "He can't help himself."

January shakes her head. "I'd be jealous, but you guys are just too ridiculous together." She turns to Callie. "Did you hear what Finn did last week?"

Mark and I start laughing as we both remember.

"No." Callie curls her hand around her neck. "Do I want to hear?"

"No," Mark and I say together.

January rolls her eyes. "They're only saying that because they were the target of it."

"What happened?" Callie asks.

January leans forward, eager to tell it, but then she catches my eye and stops. "You know what? Logan should tell it."

"Oh yes, definitely," Mark says.

I'm tempted to flip him off, but I decide against it. Callie is watching me too eagerly, waiting for this story. She'll laugh at me once it's done, but maybe it will be worth it.

"So Finn decided he was going to play a prank on me. And Finn's pranks… they go way beyond normal pranks."

"Wait." Mark holds up a hand. "Tell her why Finn wanted to get you back."

"Me? You were involved too."

"Okay." Callie is already laughing. "Now I really need to hear this story."

I clear my throat and shift in my chair, settling in to tell it. "I need a drink before I start this."

She watches me so closely as I drink her intensity could shatter my glass. I have to take a moment to get myself back under control.

I set my palms on the table and think about where to start. "Okay, so *Wired* wanted to do a story on us and asked if we could do a photo shoot. I replied back that we didn't have time for a shoot, but we could send them some good pictures."

Mark starts laughing behind his hand.

"We sent a picture of all of us, but we, uh, altered Finn's tattoos in Photoshop before we did. And um, his beard."

Callie covers her mouth. "Oh no. What did you do?"

"Just gave him a shave," Mark says. "Nothing big."

"A shave?" Callie asks.

"More than that." I'm smiling as I picture it. "We found some old pictures of him in high school, before he could grow a beard—he hates those pictures—and photoshopped his old head onto his new body."

Mark snorts. "It looked so ridiculous. And his tats…"

"Yeah, we replaced all his tattoos with trains from *Thomas & Friends*. And then we sent it off to *Wired*."

Callie's eyes are wide but sparkle with humor. "They didn't print it though?"

January shakes her head. "Of course *Wired* did. The Bastards could tell them to print nothing but pictures of kittens in teacups with their articles and *Wired* would do it. They don't want to piss them off."

"Finn only found out when he started to get all these emails about his 'new look,'" Mark says.

"Was he angry?" Callie asks.

I stumble mentally over that because if she knew Finn, really knew him, she'd never ask that.

"Finn never gets angry," I say on quieter note. "He only gets even."

"Oh, and did he ever," January says.

Although January is joking, worry creeps into Callie's expression. "Revenge sounds bad."

"Would you avenge me?" I mean it as a joke, but when it comes out, it's somehow gotten serious.

She holds my gaze for a long moment, long enough for me to almost forget Mark and January are there. "I'd try," Callie says finally.

"I'd help," Mark says.

Suddenly we're all laughing again. I feel like I haven't in so long—perfectly in the moment, nowhere else I need to be, nothing else I should be doing.

"So what did Finn end up doing to you?" Callie asks.

"He changed the traffic signs."

Callie's brow furrows as she tries to figure that out, while Mark busts out laughing again.

"Which traffic signs?" she says.

"The electronic billboards all along the 280," I say. "The ones that report on travel times. He changed all of them to say… something unkind about Mark and me."

I was both furious and impressed on my commute that

morning. And yes, laughing my ass off too by the time I made it to Palo Alto and realized Finn had probably hit every traffic billboard in the state.

"All of them?" Callie's mouth is hanging open. "How did he do that?"

"Finn is a very gifted hacker. I'd imagine it was like taking candy from a baby for him."

Callie tilts her head, a small smile playing at the corner of her mouth. I haven't seen that expression of hers in so long—fond, happy, glowing with affection.

*Keep it together, Martell. Don't break down like a damn wimp.*

"Are you going to tell me what it said?" she asks.

"Trust me, it's not for polite company."

"You should ask Finn," Mark says. "He might tell you."

That would be hilarious, watching Finn trying to explain to my wife the obscene things he wrote on a traffic billboard for all the peninsula to see.

"You definitely should," I say. "I've always wanted to know exactly how red Finn can get when he's embarrassed. Try to get a picture for future blackmail too."

"Oh, I will." Callie looks almost sincere. Like she'd love to be in on a future prank on Finn.

The conversation shifts to other things, but the easy glow lingers. After a while, January and Callie get up to use the bathroom together, probably so they can talk about Mark and me in private. Mark signals the waiter for two more scotches, then turns to me. "Callie's not like I remember her."

I tense up. "How do you mean?"

"She's... easier somehow." Mark looks up briefly, searching for the right words. "Before when she'd hang out with us, she'd hardly talk. Like she was pissed at us for something."

"No, she..." I don't finish that, because it would be a lie.

Callie never has been easy with the rest of the Bastards. Except tonight she is, at least with Mark.

And with January.

I let my head fall back. "She was always the only woman," I say with dawning realization. "She's comfortable with January, so she's opening up."

Mark frowns. "It's not like we were mean to her."

"No, but you weren't welcoming, were you? We'd talk about work, the industry, everything important to us. But she never cared about that."

Mark goes still. "Are you blaming *me?*"

"No." I'm not going to take the coward's way out here. "I'm at fault too. I was…" Holy hell, but this is difficult to say. My jaw is tight as a fist. "I was too focused on work outside the office."

"That's what you get for marrying a civilian." But Mark's tone is sympathetic.

I still bristle, mostly to do with Callie's criticisms of my work schedule rather than Mark's words. "I'm not fucking deployed. I come home every night."

He raises his palms. "Look, I know. I work the same hours you do."

Before I can reply, Callie and January come back to the table. They both look so happy I force myself to smile.

"We need to head out," January says. "We made reservations for all of us."

I set aside all my worries about work so I can enjoy the rest of my evening with my wife.

## CHAPTER 22

The warm glow of the evening lasts all throughout dinner and on the car ride home. Callie is just... luminous. Like she was when we first got together.

"Hypatia," I call as we walk into the entryway of the house. "Dim all the lights."

Instantly we're both bathed in a soft glow. Callie turns to me, her lips parted.

"How will we see to get to the bedroom?" she asks.

"I'll get you there safely." I reach out and wrap a strand of her hair around my finger. It's so long now I wrap my forefinger entirely and the strand still isn't taut. I'll have to pull harder if I want to bring her near.

I tug, gently. She resists, not pulling away but not coming closer.

I don't let go of her hair. I'm not letting go of her that easily, not after everything we've been through.

Finally she leans in. Her mouth brushes mine, soft at first, then more urgent. I cup her jaw, her hair tangling in my fingers. It's finer than silk and twice as soft, and it smells like roses.

I want to go slow tonight, to rediscover each other one heartbeat at a time.

I kiss my way down her neck, tasting the salt on her skin. Her collarbones are as delicate as I remember, the hollows warm and secret.

She sighs deeply and threads her fingers through my hair, kneading my scalp. Sparks surge through my brain, spinning away from her fingertips.

I reach for the zipper of her dress, letting the fabric peel away and reveal her skin. Thank Jesus she's not wearing a bra, like usual.

I have to pause and take in her breasts, which are sweet enough to make me ache. Small and high, with dark, proud nipples—I see these breasts every night in my dreams. I fit my hand to one, savoring her moan of appreciation.

My cock stiffens against her belly. Christ, just the noises she makes can have me as hard as stone.

I take a nipple in my mouth, suckle deeply. She tastes like salt and her own warm musk, and the scent of roses is so strong my head spins. Her hand tightens on my head, her moans going broken and breathy.

I don't know how I'm going to keep it slow if she keeps sounding like that.

*Focus.* It's what I'm good at, but Callie's always been able to take my focus and tear it to shreds.

I pull her dress all the way off, helping her step out of it. She's left in only her panties and heels, and it's so fucking erotic my cock stiffens painfully.

I kiss my way down her belly, lingering over the shallow curve there.

*She thought she was pregnant.*

Our child might have grown here, one we made together. It seems too surreal to have ever been true.

But of course it wasn't true. Suddenly I desperately wish

it had been. A child... A child would have been wonderful. And Callie never would have left me if we'd had a baby.

It's too late for that pregnancy, but maybe we can try for real this time.

I lift her into my arms and carry her into my bedroom, making good on my promise to get her there safely. As she strips off her panties and kicks away her heels, I tear off my own clothes. Once we're both naked, I guide her to bed.

She looks like a dream, one I was terrified would never be real again. But here she is.

I touch one hipbone, then the other, re-marking my claim there. *Mine. You were always mine.* She shifts restlessly, her movements languid as lapping waves.

I love her like this, where desire almost has her hypnotized.

I dip my fingers into her pussy, circle her clit. Her folds are wet and warm, swollen and welcoming. She lifts her hips toward me.

I can't resist any longer. I settle between her legs, rubbing my cock through her folds. Her juices coat our skin.

I push forward, slow, steady, deep, watching her expression.

She's got her bottom lip between her teeth, her cheeks are flushed, and her pulse thrums at the base of her neck. The picture she makes is so arousing I almost come then and there.

I pull back, grit my teeth. *Focus.* I thrust deep, going inch by inch, my every muscle clenched.

She groans deep in her throat, and my climax ticks that much closer, building deep in my spine.

I find her clit as I keep up my steady movements, all of me focused on her. The rhythm of her breath, the color of her skin as pleasure flushes through her, the way her pussy feels, gripped around my cock. The shifting of her hips as she moves with me, the marks her teeth have left in her lip, and the fluttering of her eyelids.

When she comes, I'm already expecting it. The rush of her juices on my cock, the way all of her tightens in anticipation have told me. The pulse of her pussy around me is slow but deep, and my cock responds.

I thrust once, twice, three times quickly, and then I'm gone too, coming inside my wife. Coming home.

I can't let her go. Not again.

When she opens her eyes, I inhale, sharply. Callie is so beautiful she's always taken my breath away. But in this moment, her skin flushed and a smile curving her lips, she's beyond beautiful.

"We should do this again," she says with a sleepy smile.

"Oh, we will. In about five minutes, if you can wait that long." Maybe less if she keeps looking like that. Already my cock is stirring again.

She laughs, and the sound is warm and soothing all at once. "No. Well, yes, definitely do that again. But I meant going out with Mark and January."

I watch her for a moment. Was it really that simple all along? I just take her out with friends occasionally and everything is suddenly good again?

No, it's not that simple. I wish it were. But she's made a simple request here that I'm happy to honor.

"Sure," I say. "We'll definitely do that."

## CHAPTER 23

I'm about to shatter the lovely calm of the day.

Last night was... fun. I put my hand over my mouth, holding in my smile. Why hadn't we done something like that before?

Because Mark had never dated anyone before or at least not long enough for Logan to introduce us. Theirs was always a very male world, or so it seemed to me.

Things are different now. So different that Logan is sitting in our office, typing away, completely focused on his work. But still here, with me.

We had a leisurely breakfast, then went off to our office together. Things are quiet and content.

It's lovely having him here but also difficult because I need to call my mom, which means I have to sneak away.

I get up from my chair and grab my phone. "I'll, uh, be right back."

He frowns as he looks up. "Is everything okay? Who are you calling?"

He's thinking that I'm calling Julian—the tension around his mouth is a dead giveaway—but to his credit, Logan doesn't say it.

"My mom."

He actually flinches, which is funny because I'm the one who has to talk to her. "Tell her hi." *Hi* comes out under strain.

I can only imagine his last conversation with my mother, when he told her about the divorce and she admitted where I was. She wasn't supposed to tell, not that my wishes would stop her if she thought something was for my own good.

And talking to my mom isn't easy under the best of circumstances. She's strong and determined and takes no shit, but I imagine it's kind of like having Athena for a mother. She's going on and on about all the divine intervention she's been doing and all the smiting, and all you really wanted was chicken nuggets for dinner. Like some kind of boring mortal.

"I will," I say. "Along with some other things."

Logan turns back to his computer, but I recognize it as a strategic retreat.

I make my way to the living room, curling up into one of the nooks built into the windows. The City spreads out before me, the fog gone for once.

I'd like to sketch this as an illustration—strong lines, bold primary colors, something like Mondrian but way less abstract. I want to see the people and the buildings and the cars, the life sprawling over the grid of streets.

Meowthra climbs up into my lap and yowls.

"You've got a set of lungs on you."

He blinks. I can't tell if he's agreeing or offended. I keep petting him, enjoying his soft fur and the comforting weight of him on my lap.

After a while he blinks again. This time it's accusing.

"Okay, I'll call her."

My heart is racing as I dial the number, my hands clumsy, but I manage to do it.

"Hello?" Mom always answers as if she doesn't know who it is, even with caller ID. She's not a technology truster.

"Hi, Mom."

"Honey." Oh boy, she's really happy. Probably because she thinks I'm about to tell her about the divorce. "How are you?"

"I'm good." I take a deep breath, but my head still feels light. "I'm in San Francisco. Back home."

There's nothing on the other end but her sharp intake of breath. "What? You were supposed to be getting a divorce. You went back to him?"

Jeez, she doesn't have to make it sound like that. "Mom, calm down please. Besides, *you* told him where I was."

"Because he said he was going to give you a divorce." She's not the least bit apologetic. "I thought you could finally finish this."

"You really want my marriage to end?" I ask that quietly, because hearing her say it out loud is a shock. I knew that's what she wanted, but the bald way she states it is still a gut punch.

There's a long pause. I can see her in my mind's eye— she's at her kitchen table, staring out at her backyard. She decided to take up gardening in her retirement, and like everything else she ever decided to do, she's amazing at it.

"No, of course not," she says finally. "What I really want is for you to be happy. And you weren't. *Aren't.*"

Am I happy now? I think so—at least I'm not as miserable as I was before I left—but I was also happy at the beginning of our marriage.

"Things feel different now." I turn in the direction of the office, where Logan is working. "And there might have been extenuating circumstances."

"He was never home. What's to excuse?"

I decide not to tell Mom about Logan's dad again—I've explained before, but she just doesn't get it. Having raised me entirely on her own, and also having been there for me at every turn, she can't understand how everyone couldn't do that.

I love my mom, but she's so nearsighted when it comes to other people she needs glasses.

"One of Logan's rivals might have set him up." I try to think of a way to explain it to her—she doesn't even read the newspapers, much less websites. "There were these pictures that I thought meant he was cheating, but his rival was putting them up to mess with us."

"I don't understand. Even without those pictures, whatever they are, there were still problems."

I know. I press my palm hard against my forehead, my fingers cold. I know all that. "I'm not saying everything is fine now. But we're working together on something. If he's changed… I have to try."

Mom sighs, a deep one that says *I still think you're wrong, but I'm going to let you make your own mistakes.* "Fine. When you disappear this time, can I tell him where you are? Or will you really mean it then?"

There's no malice there. Or even sarcasm. She just thinks my marriage is doomed to fail.

"You'll do whatever you want anyway." God, I sound like a surly teen again.

"No. I'll do what keeps you safe. But really, hiding from your husband for months? Callie, you needed to decide if you wanted to be married or not. You can't live your life in limbo."

She's right. I hate it, but she's right. "I've decided to be married again, I guess." I run my fingers through Meowthra's fur. "Like I said, things are different. Logan and I are working together on a big project."

"What are you working on? I'm so glad to hear you have a job again."

I perk up. "It's a website. This rival of Logan's…" I'm not sure how to explain Fuchs and *TidBytes* to my mother, so I stop. "Well, it's going to be news about the tech world, some gossip, and I'm going to ask some people I know to do columns."

I don't mention *The Silicon Wife* because I never told my mom about that. If she knew I wrote a secret blog, it would break her heart. She's always believed in being loud and proud, and *The Silicon Wife* isn't any of those things.

"Oh. Something that isn't so male-focused then?" she asks.

I smile, because I was expecting that. "Yep."

"Good. It's about time that place listened to some women."

*I'm not one of them, I'm only a graphic designer, a wife—what do I have to say?* tingles on my lips. I hold it back because I recognize it as self-defeating, and I already know what my mother's answer would be.

*Women see things men don't. Especially women looking from the outside in.*

What did I see of Silicon Valley that others didn't?

Well, as a graphic designer, I saw their contempt for anyone not part of their dudebro programmers' club. If I had a nickel for every coder I came across who thought he could do my job no problem, I'd be as rich as Logan.

As a wife, I saw the strained marriages and families as the men exalted work above all else, reaching for one more multibillion-dollar deal.

Logan never treated me with contempt, he always respected my skills, but as a husband…

We'll have to make this time different.

"There will definitely be plenty of women on staff," I say.

"It sounds very interesting," Mom says. "And you sound excited about it. I haven't heard that from you in a while."

It's true. I haven't *felt* this excited about something in a while. And nervous too, because the deeper I look into setting up an entire website, the more I realize what needs to be done. Every day the to-do list just gets longer and longer.

"I'm enjoying it," I say. Meowthra butts my hand, demanding pets. I blink at him—he's never done that before. "And I got a cat. You remember the one in the rental? He came with me."

"How does he like city life? He seemed to be a pretty independent guy."

I scratch behind his ears, and he purrs like an old engine sputtering to life. Meowthra never was an elegant purrer.

"He's taken to the high life like a duck to water. He never even bothers to go outside anymore, and he's claimed an entire corner of the living room for himself."

"What does Logan think?"

I lower my voice to an amused whisper. "The cat sleeps on Logan. Like, right on his chest."

Mom tries to hold in her laugh, which comes out as a snort. "I can't imagine. Wait." Seriousness ripples through her voice. "Are you sleeping together again?"

"Okay, Mom, I think we're done discussing this." Meowthra bounds off my lap, clearly upset by the tone of the conversation.

"You're so uptight, Calliope. I taught you to be sex positive."

"Which is great, except when I'm discussing sex with my own mother."

"Well, you can talk to me about anything." There's a pause, and I sense my mother gathering her thoughts. "I mean that, sweetie. I'm your mom, and I'm always here for you. We've got to stick together."

I pick at a cat hair on my pants, feeling my eyes sting. She used to say that all the time when I was growing up—we'd always have each other as long as we stuck together. I can always go home to her if I need to. I've always known that.

"Thanks, Mom," I say through a tight throat. "I'm here for you too."

"Oh, honey, I don't need help. I'm not messing around with some man."

That *man* is my husband, but it's useless to point that out. My mom was happier on her own, so why wouldn't I be?

"I still really like that man," I say calmly.

Which is true and also the heart of my problem.

## CHAPTER 24

Logan

We've arrived at Roasted at exactly noon, just as I wanted. When you're ambushing someone, always arrive early.

The lunch rush has already started, but I manage to snag a table for Callie and me near the back. It's got a good view of the entire café—especially the back corner—which is perfect for what I've got planned.

"I've never been here before." Callie looks around as I pull out the chair for her, her gaze landing on the hand-lettered signboard advertising the menu. Her mouth screws up in the most enchanting way—she's probably redesigning the sign in her head. "Is the food any good?"

I shrug. "You don't come here for the food."

"They why did we come?" She settles into the chair in spite of her protest. "I could've made something at home."

I wish we could've. A cozy lunch with just Callie, followed by maybe an hour or so in bed together. Yeah, that sounds way better than this place.

An itch sets up at the back of my brain. *You can't take time off in the middle of the day. You need to call Anjie, get the workmen moving on your office—*

I squash the rest of that. This *is* work. And I haven't let Callie distract me at home. Yet.

"You come here because everyone else is here," I say.

Her gaze scans the room again, this time taking in all the people. "Are we meeting someone?"

I adjust my jacket, getting myself ready for the big moment. "More like ambushing them."

"*What?*"

I ignore that. "How was your phone call with your mom?"

"Fine. She—" Callie shakes her head. "We're not talking about my mom. What about the ambush?"

"Don't worry about it." The door opens then, a group of five worried-looking engineers coming in. When I see who's coming in behind them, my every sense sharpens. "Look, I want you to be calm. There's nothing to fear from him."

Fuchs hasn't seen us yet as he makes his way to his usual table. After Mark humiliated him here in front of the CEO of Pixio, you'd think Fuchs wouldn't come back or would at least randomize his schedule. But no, he's just got to be here, same as he is every week.

Callie's face goes bone white when she sees who I'm looking at. "Wait, you knew he'd be here?"

I grab her hand, pull her up, and start to drag her over. "Yep. He eats lunch here with whichever employees he wants to ream. Tuesdays at twelve thirty. On the dot."

She pulls against me, stumbling slightly in her heels. "I don't want to meet him."

"We're not meeting him. We're confronting him."

I don't bother to smile as I bear down on Fuchs. Leave that shit to Mark—Fuchs is going to know I'm good and pissed and out for blood.

His assistant, the ice-cold Minerva, is sitting next to him. Fuchs whispers to her, and she dismisses the other employees with a quick word.

Suddenly I wish I'd brought Elliot. He could go a few rounds with Minerva for me. But Elliot sets Callie off, and I don't want her any more upset than she has to be.

But she also has to see Fuchs, look him in the eye, and realize he's just a man. That we can defeat him.

My first thought was to do this on my own, to protect Callie from this confrontation. Yes, Fuchs targeted her, but I'm the one to defend her. I'm the one to take on her burdens.

But when she came back from talking with her mom, wearing a small frown, I could imagine what they'd been discussing. The separation, the divorce, and what her mom considers to be my fault in all this.

If Callie wants a partner, then I have to try to be one. So we'll confront Fuchs together.

And I want Fuchs to know that he cannot fuck with my wife. She's mine, and his little games with his website have failed.

Fuchs looks Callie up and down in a way that makes my fist clench. I can't punch him in the face though. At least not in front of half of Silicon Valley.

"Are you here to discuss the offer I made?" he says to Callie.

He's ignoring me on purpose, trying to piss me off. It's working, but I've got to hold my anger back if I'm going to hit at him like I want to.

"No, she's not. And your offer was—"

"I can speak for myself, Logan." Her voice is steady, but her pulse flutters at the base of her throat. "I'm not afraid of Mr. Fuchs."

"Why would you be afraid of me? I offered you a great deal of money for something you have no need of. Divorced women often fall into poverty. You'd never suffer that fate if you took my offer."

His words are practiced, too even, like he's reciting something he's read and not something he believes.

"I would never allow that to happen to her, no matter what."

His attention finally shifts to me. "She left you. I of course assumed she had a very good reason for doing so."

"You manufactured those reasons."

Minerva leans forward then. "Mr. Fuchs, we need to continue with our meeting."

Irritation flickers across his face. He doesn't like the interruption.

It's odd, because Minerva doesn't seem the type to annoy him. If anything, she's his too-perfect sidekick.

And then I notice that his fingers are moving on the tabletop, almost close to something rhythmic.

Fuchs is rattled. He didn't expect us to know about *TidBytes,* and Minerva is trying to steer him away from it.

I almost smile. We've got this asshole scared now.

"Arne will take this time to talk with us, won't you?" I ask.

Fuchs says nothing. His fingers keep moving.

"You planted all those pictures of Logan." Callie doesn't make that a question. "You wanted to destroy our marriage. And when it worked, you swooped in with your offer."

"I didn't do anything." Fuchs's jaw barely moves as he pushes that out.

"You think I'm stupid, that I can't compete at your level," Callie says, anger sizzling through her voice. "I may not know how to code, but I know when I'm being played."

"Our offer was in good faith," Minerva says.

"And all those pictures on *TidBytes*? Were those in good faith?"

"We had nothing to do with that." Minerva isn't rattled, unlike her boss.

I don't care if she's upset or not—she's not my target here.

"You're using *TidBytes* to manipulate your enemies. You hid it well, but we know you're behind the site."

Fuchs spreads his fingers flat on the table, his expression going blank. Damn, he's getting control of himself. "If you continue with these assertions, you'll be hearing from my lawyer. This is slander."

"I don't think you'd come out of pretrial discovery looking too innocent," Callie says. "But we're not interested in a legal battle."

She's so cool and calm I have to take a moment to admire her. I'm not going to let her fight this battle alone, but I see now that she could have.

"*We?*" Fuchs's gaze flicks from her to me then back. "I thought you were separated."

"We've reconciled," I say before Callie can answer.

That isn't what he wants to hear. His mouth goes tight and thin. "Congratulations. Now, if you're done wasting my time—"

"But we're not," Callie says. "We're not done, and we're not wasting your time, because you'll definitely want to know that we're on to you. We're not going to let you get away with it."

The jut of her chin, the defiance in her eyes... Goddamn, but she looks gorgeous. When we get home, I'm going to tell her exactly how gorgeous. And show her too.

"Right." Fuchs has completely reassumed his bored demeanor. But his fingers have started twitching again. "Well, thank you."

I almost laugh, because that won't be his reaction once we've launched our site. The poor dumb bastard can't say we didn't warn him though.

Callie turns to walk away, tall and graceful and splendid among all these bland engineers. But after two steps, she turns back. "Oh, and I'd suggest you check how happy your writers at *TidBytes* are. It would be a shame if they were poached by a rival site."

Fuchs isn't dumb. He's evil and awful and completely immoral, but he's not dumb. When he realizes exactly what Callie is implying, his mouth drops open so far I'm worried his tongue will fall out.

Which makes Callie and me laugh all the way home.

## CHAPTER 25

After a steady week of work, my to-do list is finally shrinking. The assistant Anjie sent over has been amazing, and we've already hired a bunch of people for the site.

We've also signed on a managing editor, and she's taken a huge load off my shoulders. It turns out that I don't have to worry about every single little detail; that can be her job.

My job is the graphic design, and I'm perfectly happy doing that. I'm trying to work out the type for our logo. My efforts before now have all been unsatisfying, but I feel like I'm getting close with this latest one. The letters taking shape on my graphics tablet are finally getting close to what is in my head.

My fingers sketch as gentle as feather strokes, filling out the lines of text. There's a tall but sassy *T*, a smaller, almost winking *e*, and…

I pinch my lower lip between my forefinger and thumb and tug. Typography has been described as painting with text, and like any painter, I'm waiting for some inspiration.

My husband is sitting in the office with me, and while he's very, very beautiful, typographically he's not very interesting. Still, I can't help but stare at him. He's been working from home for a week now, and he seems... content. We eat dinner together every night and spend time together. Real time, where we're talking and not simply passing each other in the halls.

It's exactly how I imagined our marriage would be at the beginning, and I'm terrified that it won't last.

"This is how we met." Logan's voice is low, hushed. But it still rumbles through me. "Remember?"

I laugh softly, because how could I ever forget? "Yes. You stood over me just like this."

"Did it bother you?"

I shake my head. "No. Some people that hover, they think they're the graphic designer, offering criticism. But you just were... interested."

Intensely interested, both in me and the work. Men in tech can be crushingly dismissive of graphic design or user interface design or anything that wasn't plain code or numbers on a screen. But it takes skill and work and talent to do what I do.

Logan understands that.

He reaches across the desk to brush my hair back over my shoulder. I really need to get a haircut, but I keep making excuses to put it off.

"I'm more than interested." He tucks my hair behind my ear, then makes a face.

"What?" I keep sketching. I can almost see what was in my mind, the letters strong but playful... Almost there...

"Why did you keep this sweater? It's got holes. We can get you a new one."

Without thinking, I put on my old sweater this morning. If we're not going out, it's the first thing I reach for. I have an entire closet full of sweaters—cashmere, lamb's wool, angora —soft and warm as a kitten. I don't need this ratty acrylic thing.

I pull the cowl up, covering my chin. "I like it."

His gaze drops, his mouth tightening. "I can turn up the heat. You don't have to sit here shivering."

I take stock of my posture. Knees tucked up tight on the chair, sleeves gathered up over my knuckles, and my cowl pulled up to my ears. But I'm not cold.

I force my body to unroll. My marriage is becoming everything I wanted it to be. Holding myself like a frightened animal isn't going to help things even if it is instinctual.

"I'm fine. What do you think of this?" I hold out the tablet to him, although he could simply look on the main screen.

He doesn't take it from me, instead coming around and curving over my shoulder to look. His arm brushes mine when he points to one of the letters. "That one doesn't quite fit."

He's right—that *g* is too squat. I fiddle with it, stretching it, then tweaking the tail until it looks like it belongs.

"Better?" I ask.

Logan has been watching the entire time, close enough to make my heart stutter. "Yes. But you should sleep on it. Look at it on some other screens."

That's exactly my process. I probably said that to him when we were working on the Bastards logo, and he remembered.

"I'll do that." I set the tablet down along with my stylus. He's so close I'll never be able to work like this. But I don't want to reach for him, to distract him, because then he might—

His lips touch my neck, and every part of me goes to liquid heat. I don't want to distract him, but I never considered that he might want to be distracted.

He takes his time kissing me, tracing every square inch of exposed skin like he's mapping it. Like he has all the time in the world to do it, as long and leisurely as he wants.

In the entire week he's been working from home, he hasn't done this. Intimacy, at least the physical kind, only happens once he's off the clock. It was driving me crazy, being so close to him and not being able to touch.

It looks like it was driving him crazy too.

"Should we take a break?" he murmurs.

Yes. Yes, we should. In fact, I'm going to suggest that we take the rest of the day off so he can keep kissing me like—

His email pings. He goes still.

My muscles knot, waiting for him to leave me and rush over to his laptop, to deal with whatever work needs.

He straightens and takes his seat across from me but doesn't open his laptop. "I didn't mean to interrupt you."

I grab the arms of my chair, trying to bring myself back from where his kisses have sent me. "Really?"

That comes out high and squeaky. Even though he's stopped—and I wish he hadn't—the fact that he even started is amazing. Maybe next time I can get him to go further. And eventually have him never jumping when his email calls.

That'll have to be when I have less work myself. Whose bright idea was it to start a website anyway?

I pull up my web browser and navigate to *TidBytes*. I'm stuck on some of the user interface stuff, and I remember they had that Breaking News header that I hated—

"That asshole." I hiss when the page opens. "That horrible, awful…"

I can't think of a name bad enough, and I'm so angry that my voice stops working.

"What?" Logan is back by my side in half a second. "Son of a bitch."

There on the front page of *TidBytes* is a picture of us, looking completely miserable. The headline says BASTARDS DIVORCE BATTLE HEATS UP.

In the photo, we're leaving a steakhouse downtown, and we look miserable because it was freaking freezing that night, the wind in the Financial District even colder and meaner than usual. Logan has his hand on my elbow, guiding me to the car, but with our expressions, it looks like he's manhandling me.

I'm suddenly sympathetic to all the celebrities who get awful pictures plastered across the *Enquirer*. We were actually enjoying ourselves that night, but they picked the one picture that made us look bad.

"Who took that?" I ask.

"Anybody within twenty feet with a cell phone," Logan says grimly. "Which means everyone."

"I guess confronting him didn't work." As I stare at the picture, the old familiar ache starts in my stomach. I know this picture is fake, that of course our divorce isn't heating up —we're not even divorcing—but it still hurts. Some corner of my mind thinks it's real, like when you have a nightmare so vivid it follows you through the day.

Logan reaches over and closes the browser window. "It did work, which is why he's trying to rattle us. If he wanted those shares from you, he wouldn't be trying to piss us off like this. No, he's angry and he's hitting back blindly just to prove he can."

I pull my sleeves over my hands and wrap my arms around myself. It makes sense, and Logan knows Fuchs better than I do... but my uneasiness lingers. "I still wish I hadn't seen that."

I keep my eyes on my keyboard because if my gaze wanders, it might land on him. I need some psychic space between us after seeing that.

But Logan isn't letting that happen. He puts a gentle hand to my cheek and turns me toward him. The vulnerability in his gaze, the pleading, hits me right in the chest. "I'll call

Elliot, get him to write a takedown notice. The threat of legal action will make them pull the story."

For a moment I consider it. I'm definitely going to be hearing from my friends about this story, wanting to know if I'm okay, if our reconciliation didn't work out.

But I realize I'm not afraid of those calls. And I'm not afraid of Fuchs.

"Leave it up," I say. "That way the tech world will be even more shocked when we launch our site."

Logan's smile is so pleased I want to wrap it around me. "Elliot would love doing it though."

"I'm sure Elliot can find something else to do with his time." My own email pings then. I sigh, then call up the mail program. And then I start to mutter curses.

"What happened?" Logan asks.

"Another *TidBytes* writer has asked me to stop bothering them." I stare at the email, reading between the lines. "That's the third one I've reached out to, and all of them have said they can't even speak to me about other job opportunities."

There's real fear in all the emails, beyond the annoyed tone. Almost like they think their boss is spying on them.

"Fuchs is notorious for his noncompetes," Logan says.

"But they don't even know Fuchs is their real boss." I gesture futilely to the email. "They have no idea, but they're still afraid." I frown as a sudden thought occurs to me. "You never did figure out how Fuchs is passing his instructions on to the management at *TidBytes*, did you?"

"No," Logan says slowly. "What are you planning?"

Man, he can read me too well. "You said something about Minerva maybe meeting with the editors. She's not on social media... but the editor-in-chief is."

"And you think he's going to blab about meeting Minerva there?"

"No," I say, annoyed at his skepticism. "The editor-in-chief isn't that stupid, and she's a she. But she does post pictures of her lunches and coffee breaks. What if… what if we followed her to one of those places, maybe watched to see if Minerva appears?"

Logan's mouth is hanging open. He ought to look ridiculous, but he's too beautiful for that. "That… that would never work. And if Minerva did appear, what are we supposed to do with that? We already know Fuchs owns the site."

"But the public doesn't." I run my hands down my wool skirt. "We could publish those pictures on our site. Ask why Fuchs's assistant is meeting with someone from *TidBytes*. Turn Fuchs's own weapons against him. Directly."

Logan runs a hand over his jaw. It's late afternoon, and already some stubble has sprouted there, a shadow on his skin. He doesn't say anything, just thinks.

"You hate it," I say flatly.

"No." He rubs his jaw once more, then lets his hand drop. "I just don't think it will work." He rises from the chair and grabs his jacket.

"Wait, where are you going?"

He points to my laptop screen, where a picture of the editor's lunch is prominently displayed on her PopPix account. "To that sandwich shop. She just now posted that."

"But…" My mouth opens and closes like a fish's. "You don't think it will work."

He shuts my laptop and hands me my sweater. "I don't. But we're going anyway."

My lips curve into a smile. "Are you just humoring me?"

He bends over to kiss my forehead. "Yep. And playing hooky to do it. Are you happy?"

"Yes." I know my eyes are glowing, but I can't help myself. And I don't want to.

## CHAPTER 26

Playing spy with Callie is probably the craziest thing I've ever done.

We're sitting at a bar across the street from the café the editor is at, the two of us crouched behind a plant on the patio. The bar is pretty much deserted since it's way too early to be drinking. Which doesn't make us look conspicuous *at all*.

"Do you think she can see us?" Callie whispers. She's wearing oversized sunglasses even though it's completely overcast today.

"She definitely can't hear us," I say in a normal tone. "There's an entire intersection between us."

Callie makes a face at me, keeping her voice low. "We can't get caught."

"We won't, because Minerva isn't coming."

She puts her chin in her hand. "Yet you still left work for a wild-goose chase."

I did, and it was all for the pleased look on her face. "I'll have to work late tonight instead," I warn her.

"I know." Her tone is unconcerned. "I will too."

"We'll have to make sure we take some breaks then." I raise an eyebrow. "You know, so we stay sharp."

Callie licks her bottom lip, slowly. "That's exactly what I was thinking." Suddenly she sits up like she's been shocked. "Oh my God."

She grabs my arm, but I'm already turning.

"Holy shit," I mutter.

Minerva Dyne is sitting down with the editor, greeting her like an old friend. They're just meeting openly, not a care in the world.

"I never thought she'd actually do it," Callie says in a loud whisper. "But she's here. This is proof!"

I don't know that it's *proof*, but it's definitely very suspicious. And sloppy of Fuchs.

Callie pulls her phone out and starts to take some pictures, hiding a bit behind the plant. "I so wish I could read lips right now."

Me too. If I had a transcript to go with this, something more than pictures to use as leverage against Fuchs...

"Don't let them see you," I say. "Minerva definitely knows what you look like."

"Oh, so now you want to be stealthy? They know what you look like too." Her mouth flattens for a moment, but then she shakes it off.

I'm half tempted to walk over and confront the both of them. Minerva about showing up uninvited on my wife's doorstep and the editor for publishing all those fucking pictures of me.

But that would blow our cover. So instead, I grit my teeth and just imagine it. And think about what I'm going to do with those pictures Callie's taking.

Callie slowly lowers the phone, her gaze stuck on the two women across the street. "They're just so... brazen about it. How can they do that?"

"Fuchs thinks his interests are too well hidden for anyone to ever suspect," I say bitterly.

Callie's gaze swings to me. "I've been thinking we need something spectacular to start off the website."

I focus back on her, wondering where she's going with this. "Yeah, we do. But wasn't that the point of all the columnists you hired?"

She tucks a strand of hair behind her ear. "I'm thinking we'll need something even bigger. The columnists will keep bringing people back, but we need a reason for them to come in the first place. A really, really big reason." She takes a deep breath. "An explosive one."

That sounds dangerous. But also really exciting. "Like what?"

"I was thinking a series of articles on Fuchs." She gestures to the women across the street, plotting together. "We can start with the *TidBytes* stuff and move on from there."

There's a shit ton of skeletons in Fuchs's closets, I'm more than sure. I know of a few—like his preferences for kinky sex —but that's not meaty enough. Given what he tried to do to January's company and then what he tried to do to Callie and me... Yeah, those weren't one-offs. That's the stuff we should be publicizing.

Fuchs has been in the media a ton, but it's all bullshit vanity crap, wasted ink on what a remarkable genius he is— nothing about what a fucking sociopath he is.

Not only would we be taking on *TidBytes* if we did that, we'd be taking on the man himself. And get a ton of press and word of mouth too. I could already see the article spreading virally through every social media site in existence.

I nod slowly, because my brain is still churning through all that. "That's a great idea. An awesome one."

"Really?" She's pleased and a little surprised. "He might sue."

"Good." I give a short laugh. "Elliot would love that. A series on Fuchs—long form, hard-hitting—would be perfect for Greg Tychie. When we go to LA next week, let's mention it to him, see what he thinks. With his work on surveillance tech, it would be a perfect fit for him."

I stare at my wife with admiration. I should have thought of that myself, but she's been kicking ass and taking names with this media company. And it's all brand-new to her.

"What?" she says.

"It's just… you're amazing at everything you do."

She picks at a fingernail, suddenly anxious again. "There's something else I was thinking about…" The rest comes out in a rush. "I know this is a touchy subject, so I didn't want to bring it up, but I know you guys have been looking into Corvus and Fuchs. Like beyond what you've told me about. Would you… would you guys be able to share what you learned so far with Greg? For the series?"

I cross my arms and pull in a heavy breath. Some of that information wasn't obtained entirely legally. Even if it were, Finn and Dev aren't going to want anyone to look into their methods too closely.

And there's the other issue of just giving away info. We're rich and so is Fuchs—when it comes to the kind of wealth we all have, information about our enemies becomes more powerful than mere money.

We could use the information we've gathered to threaten Fuchs privately, like we did in the January situation. If we give that information to the entire world, we lose a weapon. One we might desperately need one day.

"I don't know," I say finally. "Finn and Dev might not have used completely legal methods to get it. And they sure as shit wouldn't want their name in a story."

"Of course." Callie drops her head, her shoulders slumping. "That makes total sense."

She's giving up so fast it's killing me. It's probably because she doesn't want to deal with the rest of them.

"Hey." I wait until she looks up at me. "I didn't say no. The partners' meeting is Monday—come to it and convince the guys why they should share the info. And what you'll do to obscure the source."

"But I—"

I raise an eyebrow. "If you're about to say you don't know anything about that... you should stop now. You convinced me to start a website; you can convince them to do this."

Callie needs to feel comfortable with the Bastards or least confident enough to face them. They're as much a part of my life as she is. They both have to fit.

And I need to help her when she's there.

She stares at me for a long moment, uncertainty flitting across her face. I hold her gaze, steady and secure. She can do this. But she has to convince herself she can.

"Okay," she says finally. "I'll crash your meeting then."

"You're my wife. You're not crashing anything."

# CHAPTER 27

I haven't taken the weekend off in forever.

As we assemble for the Monday-morning partners' meeting, the office feels strange to me, like a place I haven't seen in a long time. I mean, I worked over the weekend but not a full day. I... took some time off.

I'm not anxious about it. I thought I'd be eager to get back to my office, to sink back into my fourteen-hour days. But my usual itch just isn't here.

What I am itchy about is Callie being away from me. She was still getting ready when I left this morning, telling me she'd see me at the meeting in a few hours. I was supposed to be glad to get the time to check in at the office, get some work done... but I miss her.

Anjie strides by with a full carafe of coffee in her hand. "How are you, stranger?"

"Good. Look, how's my office coming along?" I don't ask because I'm eager for it to be done but because I feel like it's expected of me.

"Oh, there've been some setbacks." She doesn't say exactly what those are as she puts down the coffee. "We're looking at a longer timetable to get you back in there. How's Callie doing?"

"Great. She's—"

Finn and Elliot come in then, and the rest of what I was going to say is lost as Anjie greets the both of them.

"How was your weekend?" Paul asks with fake chirpiness once we're all sitting down.

"Don't ask Mark," Finn says. "We already know what he did." Finn clasps his hands under his chin like a maiden awaiting her rescuing prince. "He stared into January's eyes for hours."

Mark shrugs. "Jealousy isn't a good look for you, dude. Don't hate the player, hate the game."

No one's looking at me, and it's deliberate. They probably think Callie and I fought all weekend.

We didn't. We went to the farmers' market at the Embarcadero, which was choked with people, and then up to Muir Woods, which was blessedly peaceful. We talked about everything and nothing and just enough about the website to feel like we were doing some actual work too.

I got the feeling Callie would have been happier not talking about work, but she did it to indulge me. And I would have been happier not fighting my way through the tourists at the farmers' market, but she loved it.

"So you're saying that you were all sappy with her?" Finn asks Mark.

Mark only smiles. "Ask Logan how his weekend was."

Finn snorts. "I already know the answer to that. He worked."

I shake my head. "You're wrong there, genius boy. I went to the farmers' market."

The entire table breaks out into shocked laughter.

"No, you fucking didn't," Paul says.

"Yes, I fucking did, and I've got the fresh-picked radicchio to prove it."

Finn narrows his eyes as he stares at me. "Holy shit, I think you're telling the truth. And you... you actually look *happy*."

Mark tilts his head. "Are you sure? Would you recognize that look on him after so long?"

I roll my eyes. "You're a bunch of assholes."

"He's smiling," Paul says. "An honest-to-goodness smile."

Suddenly the air goes charged with awkwardness. We're men, so we don't do sincere emotions well, and the atmosphere is choked with sincerity.

"You, uh, you really do look better." Finn drops his gaze, as if embarrassed to look at me.

"I guess things are working out between you and Callie." Mark is actually able to meet my eyes, but he stutters through his words. "Good. Great."

"Yeah," Paul echoes. "I, uh, hope it lasts."

Elliot says nothing, not quite ready to be as glad as the others. It's almost touching, his reluctance to admit things are going well. He's not doing it to be a jerk—he's doing it because I'm his brother and he'll always have my back.

Dev also says nothing, but that's probably because he's allergic to sentiment. He's got no family, few friends, and no girlfriend—he proves his attachment to us by sticking around, not by blubbering over emotional moments.

"I hope it lasts too," I say.

"What lasts?"

We all turn to see Callie waiting in the doorway. She's done something with her hair to make it curl softly, her eyes are smoky, and her outfit...

I swallow hard, hoping I don't look as dumbfounded as I feel. She's wearing skintight jeans, a tank top cut low enough to make me blink, topped off with a short tweed jacket. It's hot and elegant all at once.

She raises her eyebrows. "What lasts?" she asks again.

"Our success with the website," I say.

"Oh good." She gives Elliot a look, and he moves over a chair, leaving an empty spot next to me. "I'm here to talk about just that."

When she takes the chair, she takes command of the meeting. I've never seen her like this, with deadly confidence practically radiating from her.

It's impressive, but I also like the warm, welcoming Callie I've always known. I never knew there were so many sides of her to appreciate.

"Logan and I want to hit Fuchs hard and start the website off with a bang," she explains. "So we'd like to commission a series of stories on Fuchs. Not the usual PR-heavy crap but stories about what he's really doing in the tech world."

Mark shifts in his seat. "While that sounds great, he lashes out when threatened, especially publicly. And there are innocent people he'll hurt when that happens."

"Of course I'll protect January," Callie says, quick and confident. She's more than prepared for this. "And Grace too, along with everyone else at January's company. There's so much that Fuchs is hiding; we have a gold mine of info even without what he did to her."

"We're going to LA at the end of the week to talk to some writers," I say. "And we're going to offer them the opportunity to report on Fuchs—*really* report on him—if they join the site. His involvement in *TidBytes* is going to be our very first front-page story."

Finn crosses his arms. "Nobody knows about him and *TidBytes*. Except us."

It's clear he wants to keep it that way. I can't blame him. If everyone knows Fuchs owns *TidBytes*, we lose that leverage against him. And if Fuchs begins to suspect how much dirt we can dig up on him, legally or illegally, he'll work that much harder to hide it.

"Which is why I—we—need your help," Callie says. "If the writers can access the info you've collected on Fuchs—"

"No." Finn doesn't even take a moment to consider that. "Look, I know you want your website to launch loud and proud, but I'm not giving that stuff away. It's too sensitive."

"*Our* website," I correct quietly. "And yes, we'll lose an advantage by giving it away. But with Fuchs, do you really think there won't be more fucked-up shit you can uncover?"

"I've only started to scratch the surface," Finn says. "Do you know how fucking impenetrable the Corvus network..."

He glances at Callie as he lets his voice die.

She lifts her hand. "I don't want to know and I don't need to. You don't have to give everything to the reporters, just a few bread crumbs. I'm sure they can figure out the rest on their own. Otherwise, why are we paying them?"

Paul busts out laughing. "Exactly. We can't have Finn doing their job for them."

"My name can't be on anything. Fuchs is gonna figure it out anyway though," he grumbles.

"It won't," Callie says. "I'll make sure of that. And you can have final editorial say on the finished story."

That's a stroke of genius—she's practically giving Finn a money-back guarantee here.

Finn's shoulders relax. He's definitely considering it.

They're all considering it, like she's a start-up founder coming to them with the next great idea. Except not quite. There's more friendliness here.

Finn shrugs, then uncrosses his arms. "Okay, I'll talk to the writers. Give 'em some of what I have."

"Thank you." Callie keeps her smile short, not gushing. She appreciates what he's doing, but she also thinks she deserves it. "And like I said, I'll give you the final draft to approve."

"Naw, let Logan look it over. He'll know what to cut." He grins at Callie. "Besides, everybody knows I don't read."

Callie rolls her eyes, but affectionately. "I'm not fooled by your redneck act."

"It's not an act," Paul says dryly. "Ask him how many of his teeth are false."

"Hey, it doesn't count if you knock 'em out on a dirt bike!"

The entire room starts to laugh, Callie included, and it hits me—they've accepted her. I thought they had before, but I was wrong. I never really invited her into this world, not like I should have.

I thought she wasn't interested. That she didn't have a place here. And before, she didn't. She's had to carve one out on her own when I should have been doing that for her.

I stop laughing, but no one notices.

"We're going into the investigative journalism business, then," Paul says. "I like it."

"You just like the idea of pissing off Fuchs," I say.

"Don't we all?" Mark asks.

Dev unfolds his hands, sits back in his chair. He's been quiet this entire time, but that's usual for him. Only, now he's got something to say. "I can help with contacts and leads."

Callie blinks like she completely forgot he was there. "Thank you, that will be helpful."

"Are you finally going to tell us how you knew Fuchs was seeing a domme?" Mark's question holds an edge of resentment.

"Nope," Dev says smoothly.

There's a beat of silence, stretching until it only just becomes uncomfortable.

Then Elliot saves the mood by being his usual self. "You're

going to need a team of lawyers on retainer if you're going to do this."

I have to smile, because it's so much like him to find all the bad outcomes and moan about them. I guess he got a lot of practice when we were kids, watching our dad go off about his latest scheme, which always, always, always ended up going the worst way it could.

Callie smooths her hand down the table, her expression clearing. "I need to talk with you after this about the contracts anyway. So let's discuss it then."

She's still nervous around Elliot, which kills me. But she's trying, which also kills me.

"Of course." Elliot adjusts the pens next to his legal pad, even though they're already straight.

Holy hell, he's nervous too. But he's also trying.

## CHAPTER 28

Elliot's office can only be described as old-fashioned.

Two entire walls are lined with legal books, with covers so plain and titles so obscure I'm bored just looking at them. There's no computer on his desk, not even a laptop; just a neat legal pad, a huge stack of printed legal papers, and several fountain pens. It feels more like a set for a lawyer's office than somewhere someone would work every day.

Mentally I start to add some art to the walls and repaint them too. A color halfway between blue and gray, light enough to be easy on the eyes, and for the art...

I have no idea what Elliot's tastes are. Logan is a big fan of still lifes, particularly early cubist works. He once told me he liked how it was kind of deconstructed but still recognizable.

"Do you want some art?" I ask without really thinking. It just seems so sad to have no personal touches here. "I have some friends—well, a lot of friends—who have things you might like."

*Sculpture.* It suddenly hits me that a sculpture here, nothing too big or intrusive, would be perfect. It would fit with the heavy presence of all the books, and every day there would be a new angle to look at it from. Elliot strikes me as the kind of guy to appreciate complex things.

He looks up from his papers, blinking behind his wire frames. "I, uh, never really considered artwork in here."

"Anjie never suggested it?"

He shuffles the stack in his hands. "I told her I'd deal with my own office."

"She listened to you?" Anjie is the only person who can override any of these guys. I'm surprised she left his office alone.

"Anjie always listens to me." His tone is curt, like I've confused him and he's angry about it.

I let the art issue drop. Fine, he wants to keep his office sterile and impersonal—it's his life. Even though he's my brother-in-law, I don't have to like him. I only have to tolerate him.

Elliot passes over another massive sheaf of papers. "Sign here and here and here."

I glance over it. This is the employment contract for the media company. I make a show of looking through it since I have the silly notion I might impress Elliot if it looks like I know what I'm doing.

"Everything in order?"

I stiffen at his question. But when I look at him, his expression is clear, free of mockery. Holy heck, he meant that seriously.

"Um, I think so." I sign quickly and pass it back to him.

He hands me another sheaf. He's not looking at me again.

He's my brother-in-law, but he can barely look at me. And I can barely make conversation with him.

"Why don't you like me?" I decide to go the blunt route, even though my every nerve is screaming at me not to do this. I hate confrontation, but Elliot might appreciate the honesty.

He lifts his head. "I… It's not you. But you hurt Logan."

Logan hurt me too, but I don't think Elliot will see it that way. I never had a sibling, but I imagine Elliot feels about Logan the same way I do about my mom. She can drive me crazy, but I'm the only one allowed to complain about her.

"Logan and I have some issues to work out." It's silly to pretend we don't. "But before I left, you didn't like me then either."

He shifts in his seat, then tugs down his waistcoat. He dresses so formally it's almost a costume. "When Logan first started seeing you, he was different. More… distracted. It wasn't like him, and I was worried."

It worried Logan too. I imagine that Elliot's issues with his dad are about the same as Logan's. It's certainly turned the both of them into workaholics, although Logan actually has a sense of humor.

"There's plenty of Logan to go around," I say. "We can share him."

Elliot shakes his head. "That's not true. You either get all of Logan or none of him."

I don't want to believe him. Yes, Logan is obsessed with his work, but he doesn't have to be. He can take a moment, look around, and see that we have enough. That we have each other.

Isn't that what he's been doing the past week? Seeing what we could have if he slowed down?

If that's not what's happening, if this is only him playing at being the husband I need, I don't know what I'll do.

Actually, I do—I'll have to leave again. For good this time.

I wet my lips. Elliot needs an answer, an argument, and it will have to be airtight. He argues for a living.

"Logan is very focused," I say. "But do you really think I stole Logan from you?"

His hand on the desk curls up, almost forming a fist. I've

rattled him. "He's my brother. He seemed happy enough with you at first, but then he wasn't. And then you left, and he *really* wasn't."

"Wait, he wasn't happy? Before I left?" I never noticed. I was so consumed with my own misery, I never saw his.

"He didn't say so, but I can tell when he isn't."

Of course. Elliot has a lifetime of reading Logan's cues. "What did he do?"

"He worked even harder once you were married." Elliot tossed that out like an accusation. "Like he was afraid he couldn't make enough to satisfy you."

I pull in a painful breath, but my lungs refuse to fill. "I never… I never made him think that."

It was exactly the opposite—I wanted *him*, not his money. And I couldn't make him understand that.

"Really?" Elliot's angrier than I've ever seen him now. "You quit your job, you started all that charity stuff, and you never went to business events with him. It takes a lot of money to keep up the lifestyle you were living."

I did those things because I thought that was what was expected of me. That's what the wives around here did. I was trying on that role, seeing if it fit.

"I think I should be discussing this with your brother," I say shakily. Have we been coming at this marriage from the wrong direction this entire time? The both of us?

I want us to be better than that. I want us to be in love enough to weather anything.

Elliot shrugs. "You asked why I didn't like you. I told you the truth."

"You always speak the truth, don't you?" Even if it cut so deep I think I might be bleeding.

He snorts. "No. I'd be a piss-poor lawyer if I did."

I try to hide my smile, because I don't think he's joking.

And I'm still hurting to be honest. But then I catch the amused gleam in his eye.

Letting my smile widen, I look back at him, encouraging him to join in my amusement. He *did* make a joke after all.

His mouth twitches, almost against his will. But there, there's a hint of a smile. The only one I've ever seen on Elliot —I don't think he even smiled in our wedding photos.

"So you do experience lesser emotions," I say.

He turns serious again. "I love my brother. Dearly. And I'd kill for what we've built here, all the Bastards together. If he wants you, and you make him happy, I'll be there for you. All the way."

It sounds lovely, all for one and one for all. But I've never been included in the *all* part of the equation.

"You don't think I make him happy though."

He spins a pen on the desktop, a deep frown line appearing between his brows. "You do, but you can also make him really miserable."

I give a short, humorless laugh. "Funny, because he does the same to me."

Elliot spins the pen again. "He's been happy since you came back." That comes out haltingly, almost a confession. "Like he was when you first started dating."

My back snaps straight as I suck in a breath. I needed to hear that, and I never knew I needed it until Elliot said it. He's given me an incredible gift here even if he didn't mean to.

We might have a second chance, Logan and I. Start over and come at this marriage the way we should have from the beginning.

I clear my throat. Logan isn't the only one I need a second chance with. "Do you think maybe you and I could start over? Start fresh? I want Logan to be happy as much you do. I swear."

He hesitates, long enough to make my stomach drop. If I can't get along with Elliot, what hope do Logan and I have? We can't go on with the Bastards hating me. It would tear Logan apart in the end.

Elliot takes a deep breath, his expression sagging. He looks more human than I've ever seen. Then he holds out his hand.

It's odd, because a handshake between him and me is way too formal, but also touching. Elliot isn't a hugger, but this is what he can give me, assurance in his own deeply formal way.

"We'll start over then," he says.

I take his hand, not shaking it, but clasping it tightly. A hand hug. "Good. I want us to get along. Maybe even be friends."

"You're my sister-in-law," he says stiffly. Which I guess means we can't be friends. But being real family is better.

"We both love your brother." I let go of his hand. "I hope this time around, he and I can make it work."

Elliot doesn't say that he hopes it will too. I get the impression he doesn't deal in hope or even believe in it much.

Instead, he hands me another kind of olive branch. "You're right about the art," he says. "I could use some in here. Maybe you could pick something out?"

He's not looking at me—he's gone back to studying the contracts—but something delicate shimmers between us anyway.

"Sure," I say, fighting to keep my voice neutral. "Except, I don't know what you like. Maybe you and me and Logan could go to some galleries one weekend?"

I don't know if Elliot takes weekends off. I'm guessing that he doesn't. But he might, to make his brother happy.

He looks up then, wearing a frown. "I don't know what I like. I don't know anything about art."

"I'm sure we can find you something. Consider it my payment for working out all this legal stuff for me."

His frown eases. He likes that idea. "All right then. It's a deal."

# CHAPTER 29

Logan is actually sleeping on the jet.

We're on our way to LA, taking the Bastards' private jet. I've only been on it once before, when we went on our honeymoon. There's a dining table, lush leather seats, a big-screen TV, and even a private bedroom. Most people's apartments aren't as nice as this jet.

We're both in the plush seats in front of the TV, although the screen is dark and work is spread out before us. I never would have guessed Logan was someone who could sleep on a plane—he never did it on our honeymoon, not that we slept much on that trip.

Some of his hair has fallen over his forehead, and his mouth is slightly open, and he looks so damn vulnerable I want to hug him. But then I'd wake him up and the spell would be broken.

With him asleep, I don't have much to do. My initial design ideas have been sent off to the web designers, the managing editor is handling the extra hires we need and organizing our launch, and Elliot has all the legal issues in hand.

I'm back to just being a graphic designer, which I don't

mind. But I've also got an itch to write. I've been pouring myself into *The Silicon Wife* for so long that it feels odd not to, even when I have some good feelings to pour out.

Maybe I should take Brienne's example and write an anonymous column for the website. No one can tell me no.

Logan shifts next to me as if sensing my thoughts in his dreams. He probably wouldn't be too happy about it—he'd worry about my being exposed and the fallout from that.

Well, no one knows about *The Silicon Wife* except for Brienne. I can still use it to write out my feelings.

The jet has Wi-Fi, which is almost the most luxurious part of it. Comfy seats, plenty of legroom, accommodating crew, *and* free Wi-Fi? It's like a dream, only it's true. I pull out my laptop from beneath my sketchbook—I was doodling earlier—and open up my blog.

The cursor blinks in the Title box, waiting for me to give this post a name. I want to call it "Reconciliations," but that would be giving too much away.

Or would it? I used to think that no one in the tech world really cared about me. I could write away in anonymity because no one thought about me enough to connect the dots.

But Fuchs thought about me, enough to use his stupid site to hurt me. He doesn't know I'm the Silicon Wife—in the end, I'm still only Logan's wife to him—but other people in the tech world know that I'm putting together my own site. That I'm taking steps to make my own mark in their world.

Some of them might be smart enough to figure things out.

I pull my fingers from the keyboard without typing a single letter. *The Silicon Wife* is still anonymous, but *I'm* not. And I don't know how I feel about that.

It was my refuge, but I'm not sure I need it anymore.

Logan comes awake with a start, like he was dreaming he

was falling. Without thinking, I slam shut my laptop. Then I grab his shoulder, partly to reassure him and partly to steady myself. He scared me, jumping awake like that.

"You okay?"

He blinks, looking way too handsome for someone who's been asleep on a plane. "I fell asleep." He sounds confused.

"Do you not usually do that?" My fingers itch to smooth away the hair that's fallen over his forehead or even to simply touch him in this rumpled state.

"Hell no. Who falls asleep on a plane?"

I bite my lip as I look at him. "You."

He rubs a hand over his face, his smile wry. "I guess I did."

My heart does a silly dance, because he felt secure enough with me to fall asleep on a plane. And I'm feeling secure enough with him to not need my blog anymore.

He stretches and the last of the sleepiness disappears from his posture. He's alert, focused Logan once more. As he does, he catches sight of my sketchbook.

Damn, I've forgotten to put that away. He leans over my sketchbook, frowning at it.

"When did you start doing watercolors?" he asks.

I run my fingers along my skirt, which is silk and slips along under my skin, smooth and cool. "When I was... gone."

"Oh." One of his shoulders shifts like he's going to straighten up, but he stops himself. Instead, he reaches out to touch one of the paintings.

"No one in tech wants watercolor graphics," I explain too rapidly, "and there were these amazing roses in the garden, so I tried something different."

My nerves are pinging and popping as he flips through the book, probably because the paintings are a record of when I was trying desperately to be anything but his wife. Trying to cut myself entirely out of his world.

I don't feel that same desperation anymore, but the reminder still unsettles me.

His expression is still and calm though, a reflection of the mood in the paintings. I was unsettled when I made them, but what came out was gentle, organic. It's hard to make aggressive watercolors.

"They're beautiful," he says finally. "You should keep it up."

I shrug, even as I inwardly preen at his praise. I'm an artist—I like hearing someone appreciates my work. "It's just a hobby."

Logan doesn't even have any hobbies unless you count making money. He certainly doesn't need any more wealth, yet he still keeps adding to it—so yeah, that could be a hobby.

Or an obsession.

"That was what I always loved about you." His long finger traces a petal, pink and curving. I was never happy with that particular petal, but his hand caressing it makes it look utterly perfect. "That you were focused, driven—but you transformed that into passion. And you could turn it off when you wanted."

He's focused too, beyond driven, much more so than I am. But turning it off—he's always struggled with that.

I draw a sharp, silent breath as the realization hits me—he will always struggle with turning off his focus, his obsessions. It's embedded in him as deeply... as deeply as his hair color or his eyes. It's just *him.*

But in the past few weeks, he's been trying. Trying, because he wants to please me. And now I have to ask myself: Is *trying* enough for me? Because we won't go on like this forever. Eventually he'll be back in the office and I'll be on my own at the website and then...

I don't know what will happen then.

"Is your office almost done?" I ask.

His face shifts. He knows what I'm really asking—is this magic interlude almost over?

"I don't know." Something vibrates deep in his tone. Something like… reluctance?

I'm shocked he doesn't know that, that he doesn't have an internal timer counting down to the exact second when he can be back in his usual workspace.

"But…" I lick my suddenly dry lips. "But it will be done soon, won't it?"

He shrugs, the motion sharp, lacking his usual precision. "Probably. And the website will be too."

Meaning we'll be at our deadline. I'll have to decide if this experiment is worth continuing. If I trust him enough again to keep trying.

"Yep." I wish I had my old sweater, even though the cabin is perfectly climate controlled. "We're maybe a month away from launch."

"And then we'll have to decide what to do." He finds the ends of my hair, rubs them between his fingers. "Have you been thinking about that?"

I have. Along with a lot of other things. "I've been thinking about your dad."

Logan drops my hair and falls back into his seat, his mouth flattening. "What about him?"

All right, so he really doesn't want to talk about this, but we have to. I've been thinking about the baby, the one that never was, and how Logan wasn't there, and it all seems to come back to his dad.

"He might have seemed like a failure to you… but you did see him." I twist my hands in my lap, wanting to reach out for him. But his body says *leave me alone.* "He was part of your life."

"So was my mom. And she struggled so hard. After he died, but even before. When you're the only responsible one, when there are two kids depending on you…" He closes his eyes tight for a painful moment. "I never want you to struggle like she did."

I've been thinking about that too. I take his hand and link his fingers through mine. His hand is so much bigger, stronger than mine. "I never would. If something happened to you"—God, what an awful thought—"I'd be fine. You've worked so hard, achieved so much more than your father ever did. Even if you stopped right now, spent the rest of your life doing nothing, your achievements would forever dwarf his." I squeeze his hand. "And there would be more than enough to keep me safe."

He hangs on to me as if I were a life raft. It's almost painful but in the best way. "You don't know that. You can't know what will happen."

"I do. Because if civilization were to end and your money was no good, the Bastards would still take care of me. Wouldn't they?"

He frowns like that was a silly thing to ask. "Of course."

That's another thing I've been thinking about—his relationship with his adopted brothers. They might not love me, but they do love him. They'd honor that by caring for me if anything happened to him.

In many ways, the bond they've built together is even more impressive than the wealth they've built.

I give his hand a little shake. "See?"

Logan's mouth twitches. "So you want me to retire?"

"No, of course not. You love your work. I wouldn't take that from you. But—"

I'm about to say, *if we ever had a baby, you'd have to be there.* Brienne seemed resigned when she told me about Jack missing their kids' entire childhood. I can't ever imagine feeling the same if Logan wasn't there for our kids.

That feels too much like tempting fate though. We're not ready for that.

"But it wasn't so bad to slow down, was it?" I ask instead.

He lifts our intertwined hands and kisses my fingers. I shiver at the touch of his lips, all of my body sparking to life. "You made it bearable."

## CHAPTER 30

I've hired—and fired—a lot of people in my career, so my first instinct in the meeting with Greg and Lila is to take over. This is my terrain, and I know it like the back of my hand.

But the website is Callie's idea. She's been nurturing this the entire time—she should take the lead if she wants.

"So." Callie lifts her hand, the bracelets I gave her just last week glittering on her wrist. She's dressed in colors and fabrics that make me think of the beach and sunshine, which is appropriate for LA. "We're interested in... No, wait, let me start again. We have a website."

Greg and Lila are listening politely, but it's clear they have no idea why we're here. And Callie's explanation isn't making it any clearer.

We're in a popular coffee shop in Los Feliz, the horrible LA traffic streaming down the streets and thundering on a nearby freeway, the sun powerfully bright in the sky even though it's only nine in the morning.

"Well, we don't exactly have a website yet." Callie's hand flutters in the air. "But we're working on it."

I've suffered through some bad pitches as a VC. Callie's

isn't the worst pitch ever, but she's not doing herself any favors. I hold back my urge to intervene. I won't step in unless she asks me to.

It's not easy—my eyelid starts to twitch—but I do it.

Callie claps her hands together, making everyone jump. "And that's where you come in!"

"We do?" Lila asks, politely confused.

"Yes." Callie gestures to her but seems to have lost the point she was trying to make.

I'm guessing that Callie has never been on this side of the table for an interview before. It's not as easy as you might guess, explaining the position and finding the right questions to ask. And Callie is finding out exactly how *not* easy it is right now.

My teeth start to grind. *I won't step in, I won't step in...*

Callie catches my eye, a look of pure pleading on her face. She's still pointing at Lila, but her finger droops like a dying flower stem.

Okay, now I can step in.

I sit back in my chair, settling my hands on my knees and spreading my legs. I'm going for casual but also powerful, demonstrating I've got nothing to lose here. And implying that Greg and Lila do—like, say, a great job opportunity.

"You both write about the tech community," I say. "So you already know who Arne Fuchs is."

They're both instantly alert. Oh yeah, they definitely know him.

They exchange a glance. A small, intimate, speaks-volumes-without-words glance. Greg's eyes widen a fraction —he's asking her something. Lila's head shakes, just the once —she's telling him no.

Interesting.

They both settle down, or at least try to. Their calmness is only skin-deep.

"Yes, I've heard of him," Greg says dryly. "Why?"

"I should emphasize that we are completely off the record here," I say. "Whatever is said here, no matter what happens, goes no farther than this table."

It's an intriguing gambit, and they take the bait.

"Of course," Lila says, leaning forward. "So why are you here? And what does it have to do with Arne Fuchs?"

"We're starting a media company." Callie's voice is steady and certain. She's found the thread again. "We want to build a site for the best Silicon Valley news—and some gossip. We want it to be informative *and* addictive."

"Like *TidBytes*?" Greg asks.

"Better than *TidBytes*. With more serious, hard-hitting stories than they have. We want to blow them out of the water."

"And you need writers," Lila says. She's not as intrigued as she was before. Probably because she's seen a million media ventures come and go. They've got shorter life spans than moths near a lit candle.

"We do," I say. "But we had something unique in mind for you two. You've heard of Fuchs, but how much do you know about him?"

Again they share a look. Longer, more open than the last one. Now they're both asking questions of the other.

When Greg looks back at us, confusion is stamped on his expression. "Did you hear about the article somehow? Is that why you're here?"

Callie and I now share a look.

"What article?" I ask, hiding my own confusion.

"Greg's been shopping this article on Fuchs for forever," Lila says. She's annoyed on his behalf, clearly feeling the insult more sharply than he is. "But no news source will touch it. They don't want to *offend* him, even though everything in it is sourced and sourced again."

Greg's mouth twists with resigned bitterness. "Fuchs is notoriously lawsuit happy. But some of the stuff I uncovered about him… You wouldn't believe it."

"Oh, I think we would," Callie says.

"So you've heard the rumors?" Lila says.

"You could say that," I say. "How would you two like to come work for us? We want a series of articles on Fuchs, for the front page. And we want bombshells for all of them."

Greg and Lila stare, mouths open. They look so alike I want to laugh. It looks like they're picking up each other's expressions.

I wonder if Callie and I sometimes share the same facial expression.

"Wait… really?" Greg looks like I've handed him a winning lottery ticket, no strings attached. "Even though he could sue?"

"Oh, he probably will." I brush my pant leg. "But I know a few lawyers."

"We also…" Callie stops, searches for the right phrasing. "We have some sources for you on Fuchs. Exclusive sources. But they'll need to be handled very carefully. And never, ever named in the stories. Actually, they probably shouldn't even exist as far as the readers are concerned."

Greg drums his fingers on the table. "That could get tricky. Especially if Fuchs sues and we have to go to court."

"Let us worry about that," I say.

"I suppose we could do it," Lila says. "It's tricky but not impossible."

We have them. We need to tug the line just a little bit more, make sure the hook is set—

"So that's a yes?" Callie asks.

Oh hell. Once we leave here, Callie and I are going to have a long talk about how to interview people. Or maybe I'll just offer to take this over from now on—she must have let the managing editor handle the other hires.

"Yeah, we will." Lila's acceptance is bright, almost joyous. "It sounds perfect for us."

She and Callie share a smile. Already they seem like allies.

"But..." Greg closes his mouth resignedly. "We haven't discussed any of the details."

"Salary, working remotely... Leave all that to me." I reach across the table to shake his hand. "The details are my specialty."

## CHAPTER 31

"Oh my goodness, that was amazing." I put my hands over my mouth, still in shock from the interview. "I can't believe he was already writing an article. And that no newspaper would publish it."

Logan is driving us... somewhere, his hands tight on the wheel as he navigates the snarled traffic. "You fucking—" he mutters at another driver. "I can believe it. Corvus does a lot of work for the government—newspapers have sources there. Some bigwig at the NSA calls them up, tells them he's upset about the hit job on his favorite tech CEO and... Yeah, they don't want to deal with that. Not to mention the lawsuits."

"One man shouldn't have that much power," I say. "It's not right."

I can't see Logan's eyes behind his sunglasses, but I'm guessing his gaze is skeptical. "Right or not, he does. But we're this much closer to taking some of that power from him."

I look out the windows at the sun-soaked sky. "Yep. And it feels good." I frown as a street sign goes by. "That's the second freeway on-ramp you've passed. Aren't we going to the airport?"

He must be eager to get back to work, even though we've *been* working on this trip.

Logan shakes his head. And doesn't say where we *are* going.

I cross my arms. "Well?" I wait some more. "Aren't you going to tell me?"

"Why do you want to ruin the surprise?"

He has a surprise for me... in LA. I have no idea what it could be. "No, I guess I don't."

After an hour in traffic—and a lot more swearing from Logan—we arrive at a tiny bungalow in what I think is Pasadena. The street is quiet and residential and probably filled with old money.

"What is this place?" I ask as he helps me out of the car.

"Your surprise."

When I see who opens the door, my heart stops, then slams into high gear. I want to squeal, but instead I settle for a high-pitched "Hiiii! You're Kyla Madison."

The woman in the doorway laughs at my impression of a super fangirl. "Yes, that's me."

She says it like she's nothing special and not one of the most famous and sought-after designers in the world. The only way to get one of her dresses is for her to make it. By hand.

Back when we got engaged, I mentioned to Logan—in passing, completely offhand—that I would love for her to make my wedding dress, but of course there wasn't time and she was way too expensive. And also, I had no idea how to get ahold of her to ask her to do it. It seemed like a need-to-know thing, and I clearly wasn't important enough to need to know.

He remembered. He remembered and he arranged this for me.

"Come in." Kyla gestures us inside like we're old friends.

The entire house has been transformed into an atelier, with sewing machines on the desks instead of computers, bolts of fabric on the bookshelves, and lots of gorgeous, natural light pouring into the windows. A dressmaker's dummy sits right in the middle of the living room, in front of a low couch. The dummy is unclothed, waiting for Kyla to work her magic.

I want to stamp my feet with excitement when I realize Kyla's going to construct a dress for *me* on that dummy.

"I'm Kyla," she says, holding a hand out to me. "But you already knew that."

I make sure not to crush her hand in my excitement. "I'm Callie. And this is Logan."

"Please." Kyla gestures to the sofa. "Sit. Not you," she tells me. "I need to measure you."

Logan splays himself on the sofa in the salon, arms wide, legs spread, the modern male as conqueror. And I'm not enough of a modern female to resist responding in a deep, primitive way.

He's conquered me again, but I'm willing territory.

Kyla isn't immune to him either. She snaps up straight when Logan's gaze falls on her, probably to hide her instinctive reaction, which creeps up her neck anyway—a violent blush. His handsomeness does that to women.

I'm not jealous, because he's here with me. In the end, I own all his attention and that body of his. I remember those awful pictures in *TidBytes*, of him and countless other women. How different would those pictures have looked to me if I'd been there? If I'd seen the larger context that the pictures didn't capture?

Logan flashes Kyla a killer smile. But then his attention shifts, locks on me, and I get a better smile. A truer one.

*He's mine*, I think at her, more out of pity than jealousy. But there's some of that too. I'm only human.

"In a nonpatriarchal society, we wouldn't have jealousy." That's what my mom always said. "When women are dependent on men, men become a resource. One we have to fight over. Take away the dependence, and jealousy is gone."

With all due respect to my mother, that's bullshit. I don't react with a snarl to other women coming close to Logan because I'm worried they'll take him—I react because some deep instinct says "That's the most precious thing in the world to you. Defend it."

"So." Kyla looks me over with a critical eye. "What did we have in mind?"

I blink and go stiff. "Um, I don't know. This was a surprise."

"She needs a ball gown," Logan says. "A spectacular one."

"I don't know," I say. Kyla trained originally as a tailor, and she's made some killer, off-kilter suits. "I could use a suit. Where would I wear a ball gown?"

For all the money washing through Silicon Valley, everyone consciously dresses down. The parties might be expensive, but the dresses the women wear don't declare that. Sadly.

"Hmm." Kyla puts her hand to her chin, studying me. "You'd be perfect for a modern Le Smoking—"

"No." Logan doesn't have to raise his voice, but he instantly commands our attention. "No suits. A gown. And it needs to be ready in a month."

"What's happening in a month?" I ask.

At the same time, Kyla protests. "A month! That's not long enough."

"The launch party for the website," Logan tells me. "I

want you to be the most fabulously, originally dressed woman there. And you can do it," he says to Kyla. "I'm sure you can make this dress your first priority for the next four weeks."

He means he'll pay whatever it takes, but you don't talk about money in situations like this. Funny, the more things cost as you move up the wealth ladder, the less people talk about the price tags.

Kyla catches his meaning. "I suppose I could. And for a body like this…" She circles me. "Raise your arms please. Oh yes, you have the perfect figure."

"Yes, she does," Logan says, his eyes hot and intent.

Kyla and I both blush.

"You're very lucky," she says to me, although she's looking at Logan.

I look at him too, because he's that compelling. And he always was.

"I know," I say.

## CHAPTER 32

"This is definitely not Airbnb," Callie says, spreading her arms wide.

I pop the cork on the bottle of wine I had delivered and watch Callie take in the infinity pool in the backyard and the view of downtown from our perch in the Hollywood Hills.

"No, it's not." I fill a glass, then pass it to her. "This belongs to Paul's family for when they're in LA. I figured we'd stay the night, then fly back tomorrow morning."

"Oooh, this is our wine." She takes an appreciative sip. I guess she's changed her mind on wanting a winery. "You know, this is almost like a vacation."

It is. I've done zero work today, unless you count hiring the writers, which I don't. That was basically a coffee break for me. I'm itchy about it—I'm still me—but I'm not going to give in to the itch.

Callie is relaxed and happy, which makes me want to keep her relaxed and happy. Work can wait until tomorrow.

"So you're enjoying yourself?" I walk up next to her, taking in the view and the pool. It is pretty nice, but I prefer our view at home.

Of course, the view is nothing compared to Callie. She

changed before dinner into a dress that's more art than clothing. It reveals very little skin, but it clings to her in a way that makes me jealous.

She's going to look stunning in the dress she's having made. I can't wait to pull it off her after the launch party.

"I am." She sighs and tucks herself under my arm. "Dinner was amazing, and meeting Kyla was like a dream come true."

"You deserve it."

"You know what I noticed?" she whispers to me.

Jesus, but I love having her this close, this intimate. I want to drag her into the nearest bedroom and kiss her until we're both lust drunk. But it would be a shame to waste this wine and the nighttime view.

"What?" I ask.

"No one's looking at us here."

She's right. We get a lot of double takes in San Francisco, but here, no one even looks once at us.

"We're not LA famous," I say. "It's nice."

"It is. We don't have to worry about our picture being in..." She ends on a laugh. "You know what, I can't even think of a single celebrity tabloid. I should know those, for market research, right?"

"Your target audience can't name any celebrity tabloids either. I'd say you're fine. Besides, our pillow talk counts as market research."

She waggles her eyebrows. "You joke, but the wives know everything. Brienne has been telling me all kinds of stuff. Most of it we couldn't even publish—it's just too crazy."

"Is she still set on writing a column for us?"

Callie's shoulders stiffen. "Yes. And I haven't tried to convince her otherwise."

I hoped Brienne would change her mind and we'd be spared the headache of keeping her identity anonymous. Besides, it's going to get out eventually, and then we'll have to deal with the fallout from it. Which will be yet another headache.

"I just think it's wiser if we don't have the wife of the CEO of Pixio writing for us anonymously. I mean, you wouldn't write for the site under a fake name—you can see all the problems that would cause."

She's now rigid beneath my arm. "No," she says woodenly. "I wouldn't do that."

Hell. I never should have said anything. "Forget I mentioned it. Let Brienne do what she wants. And when she's discovered—and she will be—we'll deal with it. It won't be such a big deal."

Callie relaxes, her body once more flowing into mine. "Really? You're okay with it?"

There's more hope and excitement in her voice than I was expecting. She and Brienne must be pretty good friends by now.

"Sure. There are bigger secrets in the Valley. It'll be a scandal for a while, then it'll blow over. And it will be good publicity."

Callie doesn't say anything. Instead, she stares out at the view like there's the answer to some deep question out there, and if she just looks hard enough, she'll find it.

"Maybe," she says eventually, mostly to herself. She shifts next to me, our bodies connecting from shoulder to knee.

Suddenly I don't care about the view or the wine or even the damn website. I *need* her, now.

I tilt her face toward mine, feathering kisses along her forehead, her temples, between her brows. My need is urgent, but I also want to savor her, to go slow and fast all at once.

"Logan." She makes my name the sweetest sound of surrender. Her hand comes to my shoulder, balancing against me.

Yes. Yes, I'll always be her rock, her support, the foundation of her life.

"You're mine," I say as I kiss her cheeks, her nose, her jaw. God, she's beautiful even like this, with only my lips to see her with. "I'm not letting you go. Not ever."

Blindly she searches for my mouth, her lips parting. I kiss her deeply since I'll always find her. She doesn't have to search for me.

The night is warm, but she's burning in my arms, the fire in her sizzling through me. Our kiss is long, searching, an awakening.

Everything falls away as I lift her into my arms—the view, the sounds of the night, and our life beyond this moment. There's only her and me, the only things that matter. The only things that have ever mattered.

And when we find the bedroom, nothing intrudes between us. It's the freest I've been in… forever.

## CHAPTER 33

"This is… amazing. Just amazing."

I'm scrolling through the mockup for the very first article we'll be featuring on the home page. We've been working on the site for over a month now, and we're just one day away from the launch.

And this is our first shot across the bow. The banner is an illustration of Arne Fuchs as a puppet master, pulling the strings at *TidBytes*. A friend did the illustration, and I did the typography—I've made the strings coming from Fuchs's hands turn into the letters that make up the word *TidBytes*. It looks jaw-dropping. There's no way someone will scroll past it without wanting to read the article.

The article itself is dynamite. It's the first in a long series we've got planned on Fuchs and Corvus, and it lays out exactly how he's connected to *TidBytes*—owns it, really—and uses it to malign and manipulate his enemies.

We didn't even have to put in anything about Logan and me. It turns out that Fuchs targeted way more people than just us. Thanks to the dirt that the Bastards have dug up and turned over to Greg and Lila, we've got material for many, many more stories like this.

"That illustration is fantastic," Greg says. He and Lila have flown up to SF to put the finishing touches on the story and to be here for the launch of the site, which is tomorrow.

I put a hand to my belly. That thought makes a storm of butterflies take off, even though there's nothing more left to do for the launch. Everything is ready to go, including everything for the party tonight.

My Kyla Madison dress is even here, arriving by special courier this morning. I only had time to unzip the garment bag and stare at it for a few moments before I had to take off to the office. But the dress looks beyond my wildest dreams. I can't wait to wear it tonight.

I can't wait for Logan to see me in it tonight.

"All that's left to do is hit Publish." I hide how terrified that makes me feel. I'm in command here, so I've got to put on a brave face for Greg and Lila and for the dozens of people in the rest of the office, all of them working away on this crazy idea of mine. A crazy idea that's about to become very, very real in twelve hours or so.

I check the clock, then do a double take. "Oh no. I should have left here half an hour ago."

There's an entire team of beauticians coming to my house to prepare me for tonight. If I don't race home, they're going to have no one to beautify.

"I'll see you at the party?" I ask Greg and Lila as I gather up my things.

"Yep," Lila says. "We're looking forward to it."

I wave over my shoulder as I dash out to the waiting car.

As the driver takes me home, I wonder if Logan might be there. His office is fixed, and he's back to working from there, but I've been so busy with the media company I've hardly had time to miss him during the day.

But he comes home for dinner every evening, and at night...

My stomach flutters again, with both pleasurable memories and anxious anticipation.

Not only am I launching a website tomorrow, I'm also *late.* Today would be the very first day I could take a pregnancy test, but I want Logan there and we've got this party and it would just be the worst time to do it.

But oh God, do I want to know. I was hopeful the last time this happened, but now that Logan and I have renewed our marriage, I'm beyond hopeful. My emotions are incandescent.

I have to hold them at arm's length though. Tomorrow, once the launch has gone off, then I can indulge them. Until then, I have to hold myself together.

I arrive home five minutes before the beauticians appear. Then I spend the next two hours becoming gorgeous as they transform my hair, nails, and face.

I feel like Cinderella by the time they're done even if I'm only wearing a bathrobe. My magical gown is still in the garment bag, and I don't want to put it on until just before I leave in case something happens to it.

Logan still isn't home, but he should be here any minute, and then we can head to the party together. I rattle around the house as I wait for him, petting Meowthra, doing a few small sketches of the orchids Logan had delivered this morning, and staring at the view.

When someone knocks at the front door, I race for it. It must be Logan, knocking instead of opening it with his keys because he's got some surprise for me...

Only, the surprise that's waiting for me isn't a good one. It's absolutely awful.

Minerva Dyne is standing at my front door, looking... blank. Not triumphant, not pleased. But not angry or defeated either.

I go cold down to my bones. Something's wrong. Something's very wrong.

She's got a bouquet in her hands, but she looks anything but happy. "Mr. Fuchs sends his congratulations."

The bouquet is roses, long-stemmed, exactly the shade of pink of the ones at my old cottage. My stomach flips at the sight. That seems so long ago, even though I've been back with Logan for only six weeks.

As I take the roses, one of the thorns catches on the inside of my arm, leaving a red streak. "I'm surprised. I would have thought Mr. Fuchs would be angry that I'm launching a competitor to his gossip site."

Minerva shakes her head. "The roses aren't for that. He's saying congratulations on revealing your secret identity. He loves the blog."

That last line feels like it should come with a sneer, but she just can't muster the effort for it. And then my brain catches up to her words.

The roses nearly slide out of my arms as I realize. "Oh no."

"Oh yes." Minerva heads for her car. "You should really check *TidBytes*. Like, now."

Oh hell. No, no, no. Not tonight. Not like this.

I run back inside, tossing the roses onto a side table, and then dash for my laptop. My fingers fumble over the keys as I type in the web address, trembling and clumsy. But finally, finally, I get *TidBytes* to open.

The headline that greets me is exactly the one I was expecting.

Logan Martell's Wife Revealed as Author of Controversial Blog.

As headlines go, it's clumsy, too direct. But as clickbait, it's perfect.

I thought this would be a fair fight, that it was us against

Fuchs, equally matched. But he's always held the nuclear option, and now he's decided to push the button.

I force myself to read the entire story even though I'm already feeling sick to my stomach. When I'm done, I feel even worse.

The writer didn't pull any punches. Everyone I thought I was writing about anonymously is named here. My commenters are pulled apart, their identities the subject of snarky speculation. The story ends with two full paragraphs about the launch of my media company and how it's so, so curious this was leaked right before my new site went live.

I'm livid. Fuchs knows damn well *he* leaked this but couldn't pass up a chance to make me look like shit.

My phone rings. Slowly, slowly I drag my gaze to the screen, although I already know who it must be. There's only one end to this awful, terrible scene.

*Logan Work*, the phone flashes.

This is it. He finally knows.

I pick up the phone with shaky, too-thick fingers. "Hello?"

"Is it true?" His voice is deep, resonant—and utterly cold.

"Yes."

"Who else knew?"

"No one. Just me." Suddenly I remember confessing to Brienne. "Wait. I did tell Brienne, back when I was recruiting her."

"Are you certain? Think."

He's never spoken to me like this, like an employee who's one wrong word away from being fired.

"Yes, I'm certain."

"She's the *only* one who knew?"

Meaning he never knew. I never once trusted him with it.

"Yes." It's so small I can barely hear it myself.

"All right. We're dealing with it."

The line goes dead.

*We're dealing with it.* Meaning the Bastards, not him and me. It was him and me together for a time, but now that's all over. I can't blame him for being angry.

I can blame him for not being there before, for abandoning me in this marriage, but I can't blame him for this. I had every chance to tell him about the blog, about my suspicions that Fuchs might know about it… and I didn't.

He's not coming home tonight. I know that the same way I used to know that he wouldn't be home before I fell asleep, that I wouldn't be seeing him for days.

I'm not even certain if he'll come to the party. I've made a huge mess for him to clean up, a mountain of work that requires him to fix.

And work has always come first for him.

## CHAPTER 34

I'm alone in my beautiful dress, surrounded by hundreds of people.

Kyla outdid herself—the fabric is heavy silk in a light, silvery gray, and the skirt billows out around me, yards and yards of luxury. The neckline is low, showing off my shoulders and the diamonds I'm wearing. Woven into the low collar are hundreds and hundreds of crystals, which burst with light every time I move.

I'm utterly gorgeous and utterly miserable.

I was tempted to call off the party or just not show up, but that would be giving Fuchs a victory. He's probably going to win the war, but I want to claim this one small skirmish.

And I'm here for everyone who's worked so hard on the website. This isn't just my project anymore—it belongs to all of us. Except I don't feel like celebrating, so I'm in a corner, avoiding everyone.

There's no sign of Logan, not that I expected him to come. There's been no more word from him, not even a text.

Trouble is, everyone else expected him to come, so people have been asking me where he is, when he's coming. I can only smile apologetically and shrug. And watch the speculation flare in their gazes.

Everyone knows I'm the Silicon Wife. Everyone can see that Logan might not be coming. And everyone is starting to add those facts up.

I really, really wish I were anywhere but here.

Lila and January come up to me, laughing as they hang on each other's arms. They've only just met each other tonight, but they're fast friends.

"I still can't believe you're the Silicon Wife," January says, giving me a quick hug.

I pat her back, trying not to dissolve into tears.

"It's just so cool," Lila adds.

I try to smile, but my mouth freezes. "Logan isn't happy about it. He… he didn't know."

Oh hell. Their faces drop like I've just told them the champagne is spiked with arsenic.

"Oh, honey." January grabs me for a deeper hug while Lila pats my shoulder. "It'll be okay. What did he say?"

"He didn't say anything." The tears start to leak out of my voice and then my eyes. Damn it.

January's eyes go wide. "Ooo-kay. We need to get you out of here."

She and Lila sweep me into a side room—the bride's prep area. We've rented out a mansion that's usually used for weddings, which somehow makes my mood even darker.

I sag into a chair. "It's true," I say. "Logan hates me now."

"Logan loves you," January says. "Even when you were gone, he was crazy with missing you."

My mother bursts in then, a flute of champagne hanging from her hand and a smile on her face. "Darling! There you are."

Her long hair has gone salt-and-pepper, and she wears the years of her life proudly in the lines of her face. I invited her back when I thought this party would actually be a triumph, but I'm shocked she actually came. Launch parties are not her thing.

"Mom." I take a sharp, hiccupy breath, feeling about eleven years old again. "You're here."

"Honey." She kneels next to me. "Why are you crying? I heard all about your writing that blog, and I'm so impressed."

"You're…" I suck in another staccato breath. "You're here because of *my blog?*"

"Well, yes. Why did you keep it a secret?" She pushes on my arm, her version of friendly encouragement. "It's exactly what needs to be said."

I put my face in my hands. My mom's approval is so rare I should be basking in her praise, but my life is so awful I can't.

"Logan didn't know," January says. "And who are you?"

I drop my hands. "My mom, meet January. January, my mom."

Mom waves jauntily. Clearly she's having the time of her life. She didn't bother to dress up; she's got on worn jeans and a loose top, probably having just come from her garden.

January waves back. "Callie's told me a lot about you."

"Oooh." Mom sidles close. "Tell me everything she said."

"Mo-o-om." She's way too upbeat for me right now. I need doom and gloom and little black rain clouds around me.

"Oh, I was joking," she says. "And don't worry about the blog thing. If you speak truth, people will hate you. That's just a fact of life."

"I don't want people to hate me." I don't want my husband to hate me, but I've royally screwed that up.

"Then live a boring life. But it's too late for that apparently."

"It's too late for a lot of things."

*Logan.*

He looms in the doorway, his expression as bleak and forbidding as the wind that whips through Lands End.

Lila actually squeaks, just like a mouse, then grabs January's arm and hustles them both out of the room.

My mother isn't so intimidated. She sends Logan a hard look, which he returns measure for measure. "I'll let you two to talk."

Then she leaves too, leaves me to face my visibly angry husband.

## CHAPTER 35

She looks incredible. I can see that even through the haze of my anger.

She also looks frightened. And guilty. And surprised.

"You came," she said.

I look away, squeeze my eyes shut. "You thought I'd stay away?"

Fuck, after everything we've been through, she still doesn't believe in me. Although I knew that already, thanks to reading her blog.

I should be grateful she hasn't run off again. But I'm pretty fucking far from grateful right now.

"You're hurt," she says, as if that should explain why I wouldn't come. As if I'm some overgrown man-baby ready to sit in the corner and suck his thumb rather than being a man and supporting his wife.

"You're goddamn right I am." I'm snarling like a feral animal. Hell, I *am* an animal, because I enjoy the way she flinches at my tone. "You shared your deepest feelings with a bunch of fucking strangers instead of me. How am I supposed to feel about that?"

I was supposed to fix the shit storm Fuchs started;

instead, I'd read her words, thousands and thousands of them, all detailing how miserable she was, how she was losing herself in our marriage.

And when I came to the final entry, the one that said she didn't want anything from me, didn't want to carry anything from our marriage into her *new* life, one without me...

I'm pissed. I'm livid. But I still got in the car and came here.

She's pissed now too, jabbing a finger at me. "You decided you'd rather pour yourself into work instead of our marriage. How am I supposed to feel about that?"

I shake my head. Not this bullshit again. "Yeah? And where have I been for the past month? Right by your side. You might have mentioned at some point that you had a secret blog everyone was reading."

Her face goes white. "You didn't even know what it was before now."

No, I hadn't. Because it wasn't for me—it was for all the wives who felt as trapped as she did. I still don't understand, because Callie could have chosen to be anything she wanted and I still would have loved her. And she chose a role that made her miserable. And kept forcing herself into that role until she went crazy with angst over it.

I missed all of it. Because I was too damn busy with work, just like she accused. Fuck. I'm angry and guilty and embarrassed. And terrified that she'll leave again, only this time I'll understand completely.

I run my hand through my hair. "I've seen your traffic stats. Plenty of other people were reading it. And commenting. That's how Fuchs found out about our divorce, wasn't it?" I start to smash my fist into a side table, then think better of it. "Again, something you might have mentioned way back in Platina."

She flushes with guilt. "I didn't think Fuchs knew from

the blog. You said he was listening in on my phone, that there were a million other ways for him to find out."

I did say that. What a fucking idiot I must have looked like to her, when she'd known all along how Fuchs found out. "You thought wrong," I say with deadly stillness.

"I did," she says, her eyes wide and fixed. "And now you know everything."

I laugh, because it's too ridiculous. "No, I don't. No, Callie, it's time for you to come completely clean. Time for you to confess why you really left."

I'm expecting her usual complaint about my work schedule. But she needs to finally admit that she let Fuchs's tricks get inside her head. That she let his lies shake her faith in me.

That she didn't believe in me or in us.

She cups her hand around her throat, her lips parting. There's no sound but our breathing, somehow in tune even after all this.

"I was afraid."

That catches us both up short. I never expected to hear that, and she looks like she never expected to say it.

"Of what?" I ask. "You know I'll always protect you, no matter what—"

"I was afraid of *you*." She smacks her fist against her thigh. I flinch at the thud of it. "Of how I felt about you, how dependent I was on you. I couldn't need you that much, because… because what if you left? Where would I be?" She chokes back a sob. "Hell, where was I already?"

The blog told me where she'd been just before she left. Lonely, tortured, ready to fall apart.

I missed it all. My throat closes, the trapped air burning in my lungs. She was suffering, and no matter how much money I made for her, it wouldn't make her happy.

"Callie." My voice is stripped bare. "I'd never leave you."

I can at least give her that assurance.

She covers her face with her hands, her rings and bracelets sparkling coldly. "Your life hardly changed at all when we got married." Her hands fall away, revealing her wounded expression. "And mine was turned upside down. I couldn't keep working—the second I mentioned our engagement, my boss was all over me to use you to get work for the firm. I couldn't stay."

"I thought you wanted to stop working." I suddenly realize that we never really discussed it. She simply announced one day she was leaving her job and I was happy, because it meant I'd done my job right—that she felt free enough to stop working and do whatever she liked.

"No, I didn't. I wanted to keep designing."

My mind gropes for a solution, because I want to fix everything for her, even now. "You could start your own design firm."

Her smile is sad. "I don't want to manage accounts or run after clients or any of the boring business stuff. I'm not like you."

That's not true. She's loved putting together this media company—I've seen the glow in her. "You had your charities," I point out. She certainly spent a lot of time attending meetings and parties for those.

"I did spend a lot of time on charities. It felt amazing to give back." She shrugs. "But everything I was doing was everything everyone else was doing. I was becoming a *wife*, like I was stamped out of an assembly line, instead of *your partner*, unique and needed only by you."

I've always needed her and only her. But when I open my mouth to tell her, she stops me.

"In spite of all that, I still loved you so much. When I realized I wasn't pregnant, I knew if I didn't leave then, I'd never leave. That terrified me. So… I had to go."

I rub my hand down my face. I'm suddenly exhausted,

bone weary in a way I've never been before, not even when my dad died. "I never knew. You're my wife. I love you more than anything, but I never had any idea you were so unhappy. I thought I'd provided you with everything." I lift my hands, helpless. "I don't know what else to give you. If all this isn't enough…"

I have nothing more to give her. There was the money, the luxury, and finally, this past month, my time. The time that I should have been using to secure her future.

After all that, she couldn't tell me her deepest secrets, her deepest needs. She trusted strangers on the internet more than me.

The pain of that rears up again, strikes me full in the belly. The pain buzzes through my ears so loud I can barely hear her.

"Oh, Logan." She takes a step toward me and then another. "You don't have to work harder to make me happy. You're not anything like your dad. You don't have to keep proving it. The only thing that is enough for me… is you."

It's everything that I should want to hear, but my pain is still loud. "You say that, but you didn't think I would come tonight. Why would you ever think that?"

She stops, only two steps away from me. "You were so angry on the phone. You're *still* angry."

That forces me to look at my emotions, something I've always hated doing. But I thought loving Callie would be enough, and it clearly wasn't. Yes, I'm angry, but not just at her.

"I was angry," I say, my voice heavy. "I still am. At you, at Fuchs… and at myself."

"Wait." She blinks as she wraps one arm around her waist. "You're angry at *yourself*?"

"You never felt that you could trust me with everything you wrote in your blog. You had to give it to strangers and not me. Which…" I take a deep breath, almost a gasp. "That was a hard thing to face. And yes, I'm pissed at myself for being too stupid to see what you needed, really needed, and give it to you. Fuchs didn't split up our marriage; I did."

There it is, the truth I never wanted to admit. I let my obsession with work drive her away. I wanted to give her everything… everything but my time. I thought the money was more important.

In my own way, I'm as much a failure as my father, too damn blind to see how my obsession was hurting the one I love.

Callie closes the space between us and takes my hands. Hers are small, soft, and warm. And steadying.

"No." She squeezes my hands as she confesses her own guilt. "It was my fault too. I thought being independent meant being on my own, figuring out everything about our marriage on my own. When I started to fall into roles that I didn't want to play, I ran away rather than fighting to change. Fighting for us."

It's like she's parted the fog with those words, burning it away. "Does that mean…" I know what it means, I just can't bring myself to believe it, not yet. "Does that mean you're not giving up on our marriage? On me?"

Her eyes well with tears even as she smiles. "As long as you're not giving up on me."

I crush her to me, not caring if I ruin her dress in the process. "Never. I'm a fucking idiot sometimes—a lot of the time—but I will never give up on you. Never stop loving you."

She tucks her head under my chin. "You're not an idiot. I love your focus and obsession. I'm just greedy enough to want that focus on me."

I want that focus on her too but… "I can't just stop working." I need that too. Not as much as I need her, but work comes right after her and oxygen on my list of needs.

"I don't want you to," she says. "I understand now why you need them."

She means the Bastards. "They're working on a mess back in the office right now."

"And you want to be there helping them," she says.

I do. "I'll have to go back after this," I tell her. "There's still so much to do."

"You wanted to keep working, you were angry with me, and yet you came," she says, laying her head on my shoulder. "That's so romantic."

It doesn't sound romantic, but if she says so, it must be.

"I realized I had to let go of work if I wanted to hold on to you. And I want to hold to you more than anything in this world."

"You have me," she says. "And I won't leave again."

## CHAPTER 36

I can't stop shaking my leg, and the website hasn't even launched.

My desk hides it from the office, which is buzzing in the lead-up to the launch, but I'm still embarrassed. Embarrassed has pretty much been my default state since I woke up this morning.

The party went wonderfully once Logan arrived. Oh, and we had a huge fight/resolution about our entire marriage.

He was by my side all night, using his unparalleled charm on our guests, deflecting any uncomfortable questions about my blog and how it would affect the launch, and just being the perfect partner. There was a subtle tension in him, a vibration I could feel anytime I touched him, since he wanted to get back to the office and continue what he'd left behind there.

But he stayed with me in spite of it.

I understood his tension since I felt the same way. The party was great, but we had work to do. So once the other Bastards arrived, grabbing everyone's attention like they always do, Logan and I slipped out to his office. I ended up falling asleep on his office couch as he worked through the night.

I woke up to a breakfast delivered by a local café, along with an outfit from Saks and someone to do my hair and makeup, all of it arranged by Logan. I don't even think he slept last night.

He looks rested though as he sits next to me, as calm as I am agitated. I jiggle my knee some more, wishing I had tea instead of coffee this morning. Coffee makes me hyper, but I needed energy for today. Except not quite this much energy.

Logan sets his hand on my leg, right where my skirt ends. His hand is shockingly warm and sends sparks along my skin.

I'm so distracted my leg goes still, which was Logan's intent all along.

"Everything will be fine," he says, for me alone.

I want to wrap the heavy certainty in his voice around me like a blanket. But I can't. "Everyone's mad at me about the blog, and what if nobody visits the site? What if it's terrible and I just don't know?"

That's my greatest fear—that the site will go live and no one will care. And everyone who worked so hard on this will be so disappointed.

"Greg has an explosive story that's sure to go viral. We've already been featured in several mainstream newspapers and in *Disrupt Dispatch*. And the chatter about your blog guarantees even more eyes on it today—all press is good press." Logan ticks those off with easy grace. "People will stop being mad about the blog—we'll give them new stories to talk about—and the launch will go perfectly."

"Just a few more minutes here," our managing editor, Julia, announces. "And then we're officially live."

I suck in a hard breath. Suddenly I wish I'd never done

this. What do I know about websites and journalism or any of this? What made me think I could take on Arne Fuchs?

Logan squeezes my knee, drawing my focus back to him. *He* thought I could take on Fuchs. And build a media empire from the ground up. I mean, I had to convince him at first, but once he was in, he was in.

I put my hand over his and force myself to breathe. No matter what happens now—if the site fails completely, if the rest of the tech world hates me forever—Logan will be by my side. I know this now.

"Ready to be a media mogul?" Logan asks me, his expression solemn and serious.

Oh God, he really thinks this is going to be a success. I hold tight to his hand, let his warmth and resolve sink into me.

And suddenly I do believe that everything will be fine. Great, even.

"Yep." My confidence makes him smile.

"And we're a go," Julia says.

The big screen mounted on the far wall flashes and there it is: the site we've been working on for months.

My logo is there, big as life, and underneath, the headline for Greg and Lila's exposé on *TidBytes* and Fuchs. I start to search for any faults, anything that needs to be corrected before the entire world sees.

"That's definitely your logo," Logan says.

I frown. "Why do you say that?"

"Because it's warm and playful, just like you."

Oh great, I'm blushing. "I'm not really."

"You are, and it's why you were perfect for the Bastards' logo." His gaze darkens. "And why you're perfect for me."

My heart lurches in the best way. "Thank you," I say. "I love you."

People begin to applaud, cheers breaking out. Happiness

and relief fill the room. They've done it. I smile with all of them, because they've all worked so hard for this. Really, it's not my triumph—it's theirs. I was just lucky enough to bring them together.

Then the browser on the screen refreshes and everything comes to a stop.

"Wait," I whisper, my eyes narrowing. "What happened?"

The browser screen is now blank. "Website can't be found" the text reads.

My heart slows, then slams into high gear. My leg starts to shake again even though Logan is holding on to me.

"Fuck," someone mutters.

The browser refreshes again. Again, there's the error screen.

"Quick, everyone check from their own computers!" Julia orders.

An anxious stillness settles over the room as everyone types like mad.

"Well?"

"Nothing."

"Still an error."

"Won't load for me."

My mouth is hanging open, and I can't seem to close it. I should be checking on my own laptop or my phone or doing something, but I'm numb with horror.

I thought everyone might hate it. I never thought they wouldn't even get the chance to see the site.

"I don't understand," I say to Logan. "It's already broken. How did that happen?"

"No," Finn says behind me, grimly. "It's a fucking DDoS attack. Of all the amateur, shitty things to pull…"

"Can you fix it?" I ask him. I'm no hacker, not like Finn. I'm not even sure what he's talking about. This is deliberate?

He cracks his knuckles. "Sure, depending on how much Fuchs is throwing at it."

"I can help," January announces.

"Me too," Mark says.

"I still don't understand," I say. "*Fuchs* is doing this?"

He's already exposed my anonymous blog to the entire world. And now he's trying to kill my website?

Not to mention he tried to ruin my marriage.

My jaw tightens until my teeth ache. If that jerk were here right now…

Well, I'd set Logan on him. No need for me to break a nail or a sweat on that asshole.

"He knows we're publishing a story on him, and this is his sloppy effort to stop us," Logan says. "Finn is right. This is amateur bullshit."

"Can you fix it? I want the entire world to see that front-page story *today*."

Finn snaps off a salute. "Your wish is our command."

They all scramble off to find machines, Logan going with them. I wish he could stay here with me and keep me company as I freak out, but it's more important that he help them now.

Julia comes up to my desk, looking less like a managing editor and more like a rattled employee. "I can't believe this is happening the first day." She's dangerously pale, probably thinking the site is about to implode before it can even launch.

"Logan and the rest of them are going to fix it." I nod toward them as they cut across the office floor. "Get our IT people to help them. We need everyone who can helping with this. And Finn's in charge."

Her nod is short but determined. "All right. This is a deliberate attack?"

I set my hand on her shoulder, the better to reassure her.

"We're running a story on the most secretive and powerful man in tech. This is going to happen again, but we're not giving up. The world needs to know what he's up to."

Half an hour later, the site still isn't up and I've worn a groove in the floor with my pacing. My words to Julia were brave, but with no progress so far, they're starting to feel hollow.

The celebrations have ended. Anyone who can help stop the DDoS attack is glued to their computer, and everyone else is waiting, anxious and tense, and staring at me every so often, wanting me to fix this.

I want to fix it too, but I'm as helpless as they are right now.

And then there's a shout. A triumphant one.

My gaze snaps over to the knot of people where Logan is. His back is to me, so I have no idea if he's the one who shouted.

Finn is next to him, typing like a madman, the keyboard chattering. If Finn's still going, it must mean—

There's another shout, and it's definitely from Logan this time. His fist punches into the air, announcing his success to the entire room.

"We're good?" Finn asks. "You stopped it?"

Logan pushes back from the workstation, arrogantly stretching his limbs. "Check the site."

The big screen sputters back to life, reloading the site. It seems to take forever and a day, but my heart finds time to beat only the once.

And there it is again. Our site. In beautiful, bold color.

I can see now what Logan meant about the logo. I can see the hours I spent on it, the hope I put in to it, the determination.

The entire room breaks out in applause, turning toward

Logan to acknowledge his success. But he's shaking his head, refusing their praise.

I frown at him. What is he doing?

What he's doing is finding me, his gaze locking with mine. His expression gentles, love and admiration softening the sharp line of his jaw, easing the too-raw beauty of his face.

He lifts a hand toward me. "It was all Callie. The idea for the site, bringing all of you together, the series on Fuchs... it's all her. I'm so proud of her. And you should be too."

The team turns, clapping even louder as they face me.

I let the applause soak into me, smiling as the entire team cheers me on. And I never look away from the man I love.

## CHAPTER 37

It's been a week, and Callie's site is a success.

Hell, it's more than a success—it's a sensation. We've already published another story on Fuchs's dealings—this one about him buying up encryption companies so he can break into any phone or system he wants—and that's all the tech world can talk about.

Callie's got an interview scheduled with the *New York Times* for their Sunday Magazine, a cover story about how she wrote *The Silicon Wife* and then went on to found a media company that's exposing the dark corners of the tech world.

Some people are still pissy about what she wrote in her blog, but Silicon Valley loves nothing more than success. Now that her site is taking off, most people are willing to forgive her anything.

And it looks like Arne Fuchs is one of those people. He called Anjie—actually called her instead of sending his android assistant to call—and scheduled a meeting between me, him, and Callie.

I made him come to us. He can do the walk of shame through our offices, with everyone from the interns to the partners glaring at him. Some humiliation will be good for him.

Callie is in my office as we wait for him, staring blankly at her laptop screen. Her body is still, so she's not that anxious, but she's too pale.

"Don't worry about that fucker," I say. "He's crawling to us."

She wrings her hands together. "I know, but... After everything he's done, it's hard to convince myself we've won. I keep thinking he's going to throw one last bomb at us."

"I'll catch it and defuse it."

She sends me a look that's half-amused, half-affectionate. But she's smiling, which is what I wanted.

I know the exact moment Fuchs arrives because a hush falls over the office. I'm tempted to watch as everyone glares at him—Mark's sending the dude death rays with his eyes, I just know it—but I need to stay here with my wife. And I need to look cool and composed when Fuchs walks in. I'm in command here, and he needs to know that from the very first moment.

"Right here," Anjie says, her mouth twisting with distaste. She takes off without offering refreshments.

Fuchs is right behind her, looking small and unimpressive. How can a dude who looks like such a generic dork be such an evil asshole?

"You wanted to talk to us?" I ask coolly. I don't offer him a chair.

Fuchs's gaze snaps over Callie, quick and assessing. I get the impression that he doesn't think much of her.

His fucking mistake. Give Callie another month, and no one will even remember *TidBytes*.

I cross my arms. Maybe I should throw him out right now, not let him back in until he treats my wife with the proper respect.

Fuchs's cold gaze lands on me, and his mouth tightens. "I'm selling *TidBytes*. I wanted to give you the first chance to make an offer."

Callie gasps. I'm as shocked as she is, but I know better than to show it.

"Really?" I drawl, as if I couldn't care less.

"You're selling?" Callie asks, her mouth wide.

"Thanks to your *website*"—Fuchs practically spits the word out—"*TidBytes* is now useless to me."

I snort. Of course he's here to get some kind of advantage for himself. "And here I thought you'd be apologizing to us. If it's useless to you, why should I buy it rather than leaving it hanging around your neck?"

I'd love to see it choke him, although *TidBytes*'s budget is a drop in the massive bucket that is Fuchs's fortune. Sadly, he won't go broke from one failing website.

Fuchs's mouth turns up into something too nasty to be a smile. "Because if you don't, I'll fire every single employee and purge all the archives."

"Oh." That's caught at Callie's heart—she wants to save all those employees.

Which means I'll have to save them now. I can't have my wife thinking I'm a heartless brute.

"I'll hire them once you've fired them," I say with a shrug. "Hell, I'm already recruiting a dozen of them right now."

They're all too afraid of his lawyers to accept an interview, but I imagine they'll get over it once they hear the site is going under.

Fuchs's face turns a dangerous shade of red, the kind a bull would charge at. I keep looking bored, even though I'm inwardly cheering. Asshole thinks he can come in here and strong-arm us? Yeah, no fucking way.

"They can't be hired by you," he finally gets out. "Their noncompete won't allow it."

"Contracts are void once the company goes under." I move toward the door since I'm ready for this farce to be over.

"Why is it useless to you?" Callie's expression says she doesn't expect him to answer, but she has to ask anyway.

I pause on my way to the door. "Because everyone knows he's behind every single slimy story on the site. That he's only publishing that crap to manipulate people. And it's hard to manipulate people when they know who's pulling the strings."

Fuchs's expression goes stony, meaning I've hit it right on the head. And he still won't acknowledge Callie.

"If you won't buy it," he says, "someone else will."

He's out of tricks if he's pulling that one.

"No, they won't," I say. "Media properties are a dime a dozen. And who'd want to go up against my wife's site with a tainted brand like *TidBytes*? Better to start fresh." I pull open my office door, inviting him to take his evil ass right through it. "You've lost, Fuchs. Again."

"I'll make sure everyone in this town reads your wife's blog and sees everything she wrote about them behind their back."

Callie's expression is stricken. I silently curse all the jerks who've been shitty to her about that blog.

"Good," I say. "My wife has excellent insights. She said things that needed saying."

"Logan." Callie twists my name into delighted shock.

I raise one eyebrow in a shrug, because everything I've said is true.

"It will be a scandal." Fuchs practically snarls that.

Finally I take hold of his arm and push him through the door. I've had enough and so has Callie.

"I'm a Bastard," I say. "I eat scandal for breakfast. And if

you come after my wife or my marriage again, I'll break
more than just your toy website this time—I'll break *you.*"

## CHAPTER 38

*Wow.*

I know I should say something, but all I can think is *wow.*

"You just slammed the door on Arne Fuchs."

Okay, I'm stating the obvious here, but still. I can hardly believe what I've just seen. Or what I've just heard.

Logan thinks everyone should read my blog. He thinks I said things that needed to be said.

And Fuchs is selling *TidBytes.* He's abandoning it.

"I should have tossed him out the moment he offered *TidBytes* to us." Logan dusts off his hands as if he's just finished a job well done. Which I suppose he has. "But at least that's out of the way."

Logan throws himself into his desk chair, all negligent sprawl. He looks like an ad for a high-end cocktail. *Come enjoy me at the end of the day.*

I'm the lucky girl who'll get to.

He pats his leg, his gaze darkening. "Come here. I need to tell you something."

This sounds promising. And exciting.

"Oh?" I slink over to him, desire sliding through my

limbs, making me loose with heat. "Is it safe to talk about at work?"

His smile is knowing. "Yes."

I pout as I fold myself into his arms. "That doesn't sound as fun as what I was imagining."

Instead of teasing me back, he wraps me up tight, his chest solid against my back, his arms lashed around my rib cage, his chin tucked into my hair. We breathe together for several long, lovely moments.

"You did it," he says, breaking the silence. "You wanted to stop Fuchs, and you did. *TidBytes* is done."

I ponder that, turning it over in my mind. Yes, that was my original goal—at least that's what I told myself. "Yes, and that's a good thing… but I think what I really wanted was you back. Only I couldn't quite admit it or see how to make it happen."

I hear him swallow. "I was stupid and blind. I won't make that mistake again."

"They say the only way you learn anything is by making mistakes." I turn so that I'm nestled against his chest. "I'd say we've learned quite a bit here. And I've made more than my share here too. Like the blog."

His arms tighten. "The blog wasn't a mistake. That's what I wanted to talk to you about—you should keep doing the blog. Only as a column on the website, under your real name."

That's so unexpected all I can do is blink. "But…"

I'm about to say *I'm not a real writer*, but I close my mouth on it. Because I've also never built a media company before or thwarted an evil mastermind, but somehow I managed to do both of those in the past month.

"But what?" Logan prompts. "People loved the blog. So keep it going. And it would bring traffic to the site."

I set my hand on his flat stomach, spreading my fingers

wide. Through the thin cotton of his shirt, I can feel the warmth of his skin, the bunch and give of his muscles. Lord, but his body is distracting.

"So this is all about site traffic?" I grin at him.

"No." His voice drops. "But you share things there other people need to hear. People like you who feel lost in this world. And people like me who sometimes can't see those who feel lost."

My eyes prickle and I blink hard. "How can I say no when you put it like that?"

He wraps his fingers around my wrist. "You can always say no. But I think you need that outlet."

"There will probably be a scandal," I warn him. But he's right—I *do* want to keep writing *The Silicon Wife*. It will be different from what I was writing before since I'm in a different place in life, but I still have a lot to say about Silicon Valley.

"I eat scandal for breakfast, remember?" He nuzzles my ear, tickling me with his voice.

"That's right." I lift my face to his and am rewarded with a kiss. "I guess I'd better do it then and make some more scandal for you."

His laugh is dark and sensual but nothing compared to his kiss. I could do this forever, just lose myself in him.

"God, I wish I could drag you home right now," he mutters against my lips. His cock is pressing against my ass, proving how badly he wishes it.

Then I remember the thing I forgot. The thing that was occupying my mind before the launch, that got lost in the lawsuit and my unmasking and the almost-failed launch.

Oh my God, of all the things to lose in that mess…

Chills are running over my skin. "We need to go home."

He's instantly alert. "What's wrong?"

"I… I forgot something." It's happening all over again, the

hope, the fear, the sense that everything will change. "Please can we go home? Now?"

I know he needs to work, and I need to work, but I have to know, right now. And I need him with me when I do.

"Can we…?" He stops when I keep staring at him pleadingly. His jaw tightens, his gaze cutting away. "Okay," he says heavily. "We'll go home and get whatever you need."

This is hard for him, leaving work in the middle of the day, and I haven't even explained to him what's really going on. But he helps me up and rises from his chair, all without reluctance.

I said that I need him, and he's coming. The hope in my heart burns so strong it almost hurts.

## CHAPTER 39

As soon as I shut the front door, I ask, "Okay, what's really going on?"

During the entire drive up the 280, Callie refused to tell me why we were racing home. She did promise to tell me once we were inside, and now that we are, I want some answers.

She looks okay—hell, she looks amazing—but something serious is going on. If she doesn't tell me what it is, I can't fix it.

She clasps her hands together as she stops in the foyer, her eyes wide. "I don't know how to tell you this, and I feel like such a fool."

I know she's not leaving me, not again, but my heart kicks with adrenaline anyway. This can't be good, not when it's starting like this—

"I think I'm pregnant."

"What?" I didn't mean to yell, but the bottom is dropping out from under me. "Why didn't you tell me sooner?"

"I, um, forgot. I was late the night of the launch and was going to tell you then, and everything happened and I forgot all about it until today, and that's why I feel silly."

I grab her and spin her around, because she's just that amazing and I can't think of any other way to show her how I feel. "Oh my God. I thought something was wrong."

She sets her forehead against mine. "So you're not upset?"

"God, no." Suddenly I realize what I'm doing. I set her down quickly. "Shit, did I hurt you? You need to see a doctor, right away. We'll have to find someone at Stanford. No, UCSF—they're better."

She's laughing, and I don't understand why. "Logan." She puts her hand in the center of my chest. "I haven't even taken the at-home test yet. I don't even know if I really am."

I hold up my keys. "I can be to the drugstore and back in twenty minutes. What kind do you want? Never mind, I'll get some of each. Can't be too careful—"

Her hand flexes on my sternum. "I already have a test. From last time."

My breath catches. I don't want to remember her leaving. But that painful past is still part of us. The pain makes the happiness we share now that much sweeter.

"Okay," I say. "What should I do?"

"Just… just wait for me."

"Always."

I feel like an expectant father trapped in the fifties as I wait outside the bathroom door for Callie. She's in there taking the pregnancy test, and I'm stuck out here, feeling useless.

And yeah, a little proud. She might have a baby, thanks to me. Hey, a man's allowed to be pleased when he's impregnated his wife, as long as he's not a dick about it.

I jiggle my leg, biting back the urge to ask her if everything's okay. Peeing on a stick isn't exactly dangerous.

But… it also kind of is. Everything in our lives will change if the test is positive. We won't just be married—we'll be parents.

Finally I can't hold back. I think my heart might explode with waiting. "Honey?"

"Sorry." When she opens the door, her eyes are wide, her breath coming too quick. She's nervous too. "It's ready, but it takes a couple of minutes."

She links her fingers deeply in mine, and we walk into the bathroom together.

The stick is sitting in the sink, looking way too innocent for what it's about to tell us. I had no idea pregnancy tests were so plain. This is a big fucking deal. Shouldn't there be more?

I should have gone to the drugstore. I still can.

I squint at the stick. "Is that…? What does that mean?"

There might be a very faint line there, but I can't quite tell. It's there one second, gone the next. What a shitty trick to play on someone taking a pregnancy test.

And then— "Oh shit." My heart is hammering against my ribs.

Callie's hand tightens on mine. "It's only the test line."

"Way to give me a fucking heart attack," I mutter.

She snickers.

Another line starts to form. Maybe.

I hold my breath tight, as tightly as I'm holding Callie's hand, wishing and praying.

"Is it really there?" I whisper.

Her swallow is loud, but her answer is quiet. "I think so."

"What… what does it mean?" I was thinking the second line meant the test is positive, but Callie isn't reacting, and now I don't know.

"It means…" She takes a deep breath that goes shaky at the very end. "It means yes."

"Yes?" Suddenly that word is more than just a word. It's the rest of our life, together. Loving each other and our child.

Callie nods, then covers her mouth, a wild laugh bursting out of her. "Yes. Yes, yes, yes."

I pull her into my body, cover her with the curve of mine. Covering her and the child inside her. Our child.

I try to think of something to say, words that will encompass this moment and how I feel about her and our future child. About how I'll always be here for her, always trying to be better because that's what they both deserve.

But all I can say is "I love you."

When she says, "I love you too," those simple words feel like more than enough.

## CHAPTER 40

I didn't fully appreciate the winery Logan bought me the first time I saw it.

Back then it felt like a bandage over a wound that needed stitches or even surgery—Logan couldn't see that I was badly, badly hurt and he was only offering a token bit of comfort.

Things are very different now.

I put my hand on my belly as I take in the massive two-story entry, with parquet tiles on the floor and scrollwork banisters and skylights. The entire sensation is one of light—both illumination and weightlessness.

"Not bad for a weekend house?" Logan says as he brings in our bags.

"That's one way to put it." I'm too awed by the place to say anything more.

We've decided that as a way to slow down, we'll be spending the weekends up here in Napa, at our winery. We'll be mostly cut off from the rest of the world, and we definitely won't be working.

"How are you feeling?" Logan asks, pressing a kiss to my forehead.

He only asks me that every five minutes every day. And he races home by five each night in order to make me a home-cooked meal. He's also been to every doctor's appointment, not that we've had a ton. I'm only five months along, and everything is going well so far, so they don't need to see me that often.

Logan wasn't happy to hear about the appointment schedule and wanted to find a doctor who'd see me once a week. I managed to talk him out of that—barely.

"I'm fine." I rub the tiny swell of my belly. "Although I'm kind of hungry."

"Let me see what's in the kitchen." He's already halfway across the entry when his phone buzzes. He fishes it out of his jacket pocket. "It's Mark, texting me. Do you mind?"

I'm so touched that he's asking if it's okay. "Sure."

As he reads the text, he starts to laugh. "Oh, you'll love this." He turns the phone so I can see what he's looking at. "*TidBytes* is closing."

There's a story right there on *Disrupt Dispatch*, announcing that *TidBytes* will be shutting down, capped off with an awful picture of Arne Fuchs.

I shake my head. "That's too bad. I bet their writers will be looking for new jobs soon."

Fuchs made good on his threat then. Logan kept to his promise to never spend a dime for *TidBytes,* and it looked like no one else in the Valley wanted it either.

Why would they? My site is kicking *TidBytes*'s butt every day. It would be a bad investment. No one seems to want to give Arne Fuchs any money at the moment.

He lost a lot of face when the stories about him came out on our site. He didn't give a public statement about it, but I imagine he was furious. And now his gossip rag is gone too. I'm sure he's furious with *me*, personally.

But I've got Logan and the Bastards in my corner. Let him come at me.

We'll hire the best of their writers and keep moving forward with our media company. And Fuchs will have to find some other way to play his nasty games.

I'm sure he'll come up with something, and we'll have to be ready for it. But for now I'm going to enjoy my winery.

Logan is still staring at his phone.

"Are you going to be okay with this?" I ask. "Leaving work for so long?"

He blinks like he's coming out of a dream. Then he turns the phone all the way off and sets it on the entryway table. "I'll be fine. Work will still be there when I get back—they can't fire me—and everything I need is right here with you." He takes my hand. "My entire focus is going to be on you from now on. Let's find you something to eat."

I can't argue with any of that.

## ABOUT THE AUTHOR

Raleigh fell in love with billionaire romance as a teenager thanks to Harlequin Presents. She fell in love with San Francisco in her twenties thanks to how charming the city was. And she fell for a coding genius thanks to how charming *he* was.

Naturally, she had to put all of the things she loved into her romances.

You can find her online at www.raleighdavis.com.